THE FLYING
DINOSAURS

The Illustrated Guide to
the Evolution of Flight

Philip J. Currie
Illustrations by Jan Sovak

Red Deer College Press

DISCOVERY BOOKS ARE PUBLISHED BY
Red Deer College Press
56 Avenue & 32 Street Box 5005
Red Deer Alberta Canada T4N 5H5

CREDITS
Design by Boldface Technologies Ltd.
Typesetting by Boldface Technologies Ltd.
Colour Separation by Colour Four Graphics Ltd.
Printed and bound in Singapore for Red Deer College Press
by Kyodo Printing Co. Pte. Ltd.

CANADIAN CATALOGUING IN PUBLICATION DATA
Currie, Philip J., 1949-
The flying dinosaurs
Includes index
ISBN 0-88995-078-4
1. Dinosaurs. I. Sovak, Jan, 1953-
II. Title.
QE862.D5C87 1991 567.9'1 C91-091243-2

Acknowledgments

Both the author and artist would like to express gratitude for the support of their families. Marlene Currie and Daniela Sovak patiently monitored all the late nights and weekends necessary to complete this project. We also thank Dennis Johnson of Red Deer College Press, who suggested the book initially, and whose enthusiastic support carried the project to its completion.

In recent years, we have seen a tremendous revival in interest in not only dinosaurs, but in many other groups of fossil reptiles as well. Over the years, the author has served with numerous expeditions that collected pterosaur, dinosaur and bird material in Canada and China, and has had opportunities to look at thousands of specimens in museums and universities around the world. It has been the author's pleasure to work with Kevin Padian (University of California at Berkeley) and Dale Russell (Canadian Museum of Nature, Ottawa) on pterosaur material from Alberta. His interest in pterosaurs has also been inspired by other colleagues, most notably Nataly Bakhurina (Paleontological Institute, Moscow), Christopher Bennet (University of Kansas, Lawrence), Wann Langston, Jr. (University of Texas, Austin), David Unwin (University of Reading, England), Peter Wellnhofer (Bayerische Staatssammlung fur Palaontologie und historische Geologie, Munich), and Rupert Wild (Staatliches Museum fur Naturkunde, Stuttgart). The author's field of expertise is dinosaurs, especially the carnivorous theropods so closely related to the origin of birds. Robert T. Bakker (University of Colorado at Boulder), Kenneth Carpenter (Denver Museum of Natural History), Dong Zhiming (Institute of Vertebrate Paleontology and Paleoanthropology, Beijing), Greg Paul (Baltimore), Antangerel Perle (Paleontological Institute of Mongolia, Ulaan Baatar) and Dale Russell (Canadian Museum of Nature, Ottawa) had a direct influence on the dinosaurs selected for this volume. Sankar Chatterjee (Texas Tech University, Lubbock), Sergai Kurzanov (Paleontological Institute, Moscow), Larry Martin (University of Kansas, Lawrence), John Ostrom (Yale University, New Haven), Paul Sereno (University of Chicago), Sam Tarsitano (Texas) and Peter Wellnhofer freely discussed material included in the bird section.

–PHILIP J. CURRIE AND JAN SOVAK

The Publishers gratefully acknowledge the financial contribution of the Canada Council, the Alberta Foundation for the Arts, Alberta Culture and Multiculturalism, Red Deer College and Radio 7 CKRD.

Contents

Foreword

Today, as we jet all over the world and fly to the moon, it's hard to imagine we ever could have been a completely grounded species. Before we invented flying machines, all we could do was to look up and wonder at the powers of the birds and bats, and their mastery of the air. It's interesting to reflect that when aerodynamicists first started to invent flying machines, they looked for inspiration to flying animals. With the evolution of the aircraft industry and more sophisticated aerodynamics, the tables were turned: we now use what we know about principles of flight design to analyze the skills of birds, bats and pterosaurs.

In this book you will learn about many reptilian fliers from Dr. Philip Currie, one of our foremost dinosaurian palaeontologists. He has spent a long time puzzling over dinosaur bones and footprints from the Cretaceous of Canada, China and the United States, and has distinguished himself by solving many problems in the palaeontology of ancient reptiles. You'll notice when I said "reptiles," I did not say "and birds." The reason is that we now know birds are descended from small carnivorous dinosaurs, such as the ones Dr. Currie has studied so intensively. So, in one sense, to the taxonomist, birds are members of the Dinosauria, and we can learn much about the origin of flight in birds by looking at their closest dinosaurian relatives.

Pterosaurs, of course, were also true reptiles. They were the closest major group of reptiles to the dinosaurs and also the first flying vertebrates to flap their wings actively. The distinction between flapping and gliding is important. A gliding animal of today, such as a gliding squirrel, uses flight to escape predators, perhaps, or to save energy by coasting through the air from one tree to the next. But a true flapping animal can do much more on the wing: it can look for food, trap prey and even mate in the air. The transition from gliding to flapping is not well understood, and some ancient flapping groups may never have evolved through a gliding stage. But any way you look at it, the origin of flight is a really important example of how big changes in evolution take place. The best way we can study it is to look carefully at the kinds of animals today, and in the past, that use flight in all its various forms: parachuting, gliding, flapping and soaring. The excitement of vertebrate flight has lasted over 250 million years, and it continues.

–KEVIN PADIAN
  CURATOR, MUSEUM OF PALEONTOLOGY
  UNIVERSITY OF CALIFORNIA, BERKELEY

Introduction

Like many children, my fascination with prehistoric life began when I discovered dinosaurs. Initially, I thought all extinct animals were dinosaurs, but I soon learned otherwise. Mammoths and mastodons were elephants, not dinosaurs. The giant amphibians living in the Palaeozoic swamps of 300 million years ago were not dinosaurs either. Even the gigantic marine reptiles and the great flying reptiles of the Mesozoic were not dinosaurs, although they at least were contemporaries. In fact, as I was growing up, even the term *Dinosauria* was dropped from usage as scientists realized the name encompassed two distinct lineages of animals that did not appear to be closely related. Although *dinosaur* continued as a popular term, the animals were classified either as saurischians (lizard-hipped dinosaurs) or ornithischians (bird-hipped dinosaurs).

Recent study has demonstrated that the Saurischia and Ornithischia still had much in common. They were united by both a common ancestor and a suite of characteristics. The name *Dinosauria* was appropriately resurrected before its 150th anniversary in 1991.

The word *dinosaur*, coined by Sir Richard Owen in 1841, means "Terrible Lizard." Not every dinosaur was terrible, and none was a lizard, but the name has a certain romantic appeal. But dinosaur is just a word, and the classification of animals is only an elaborate filing system invented by humans. Animals do share different degrees of relationship, and a good classification system will show us how living organisms are interrelated. But there are different classification systems, just as there are different filing systems in an office.

Until recently, scientists classified into units plants and animals generally similar to each other. Each unit, or taxon, had a name. This classification system worked well for several centuries, although it had some shortcomings. For example, at one time, two primitive reptile species might have been considered members of the same family if they had generally similar characteristics.

However, most of these characters may have been primitive and therefore found in a wide variety of animals. And although the two reptiles in our example looked almost the same, a few very specialized characters showed one was already evolving into a mammal, and the other had taken the first evolutionary step toward dinosaurs and birds. Perhaps, then, it would be more meaningful to classify these two similar-looking reptiles into two distinct families grouped with their very different-looking descendants.

A new system of classification, called either cladistics or phylogenetic systematics, does just that. This type of classification, gaining wide recognition in recent years, groups living organisms by the derived, advanced or specialized characteristics they share. Derived characters are more important than all the general similarities because once specialized features develop, they tend to be passed on to descendants and can be traced through many generations. Dinosaurs share a suite of almost a dozen derived characters not found in any other animals except birds. Most of these dinosaurian characters resulted from improvements in dinosaurs' ability to walk and run. Did these advanced features evolve independently in dinosaurs and birds? Or did one creature evolve from the other?

A cladogram is like a family tree, but each new branch marks the appearance of a new character shared by all animals farther out on the limb. This simplified cladogram shows how birds, dinosaurs and pterosaurs are related to other more familiar reptiles.

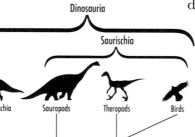

Dinosauria

Saurischia

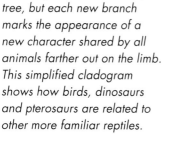

Turtles Lizards Snakes Crocodiles Pterosaurs Ornithischia Sauropods Theropods Birds

On the surface, it's hard to connect what we think of as lumbering, scaly, cold-blooded prehistoric dinosaurs with tiny, feathered hot-blooded fliers. But under a cladistic classification, birds are a subset of the Dinosauria. That's right! Birds, as the direct descendants of meat-eating dinosaurs, called the theropods, can be classified as dinosaurs. At one time, when we believed dinosaurs were slow, cold-blooded, solitary and stupid, such a statement may have been considered heresy. But over the last few decades, a renaissance in research on dinosaurs has provided insight into why these creatures were so successful for so long, and the stereotype has been supplanted by agile, warm-blooded, intelligent forms more in keeping with our image of birds. Dinosaurs are not extinct, but are represented today by thousands of species. From the miniscule hummingbird to the fiercest eagle, the children of dinosaurs inhabit every corner of our world.

Under our current cladistic classification system, another branch of flying creatures, the flying reptiles known as pterosaurs, are not considered dinosaurs. But they were closely related to both dinosaurs and birds. Once, scientists even considered the possibility that pterosaurs were the ancestors of birds. This now appears unlikely. Other research suggests pterosaurs were more closely related to meat-eating dinosaurs than to plant-eating forms, and it is conceivable flying reptiles eventually may be classified as offshoots of the theropods too.

This book focuses on these two closely related groups of flying animals – pterosaurs and their cousins, those dinosaurs we call birds. It would be difficult to describe all types of pterosaurs and birds in a single book, so it has been necessary to make a selection of species. The pterosaurs selected represent the widest range of variation known, and references are made to similar forms. Carnivorous dinosaurs relevant to the origin of birds have been included. Links between the two are often so close that scientists have difficulty determining if certain fossils are from theropod dinosaurs or birds. The suggestion has even been made that some of the last meat-eaters were actually birds that had reversed the evolutionary process and gone back to living on the ground. The birds selected represent the earliest known species and some of the more spectacular forms from later times.

Pterosaurs, theropods and birds all lived during the Mesozoic, an era spanning more than 180 million years. What a fantastic time that must have been! Imagine sitting at the edge of a forest and looking across a marshy plain dotted by horned dinosaurs feeding on ferns and cycads, preparing for their annual migration north into the Arctic Circle. There is no grass, but most of the other plants look astonishingly modern. As you listen to the singing of birds in the trees and bushes, a shadow races along the ground, and you glance up to see a pterosaur the size of a small airplane soaring overhead!

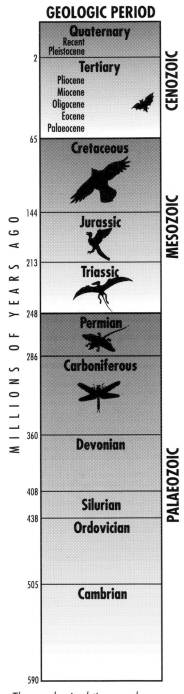

The geological time scale was devised by geologists and palaeontologists to characterize major events in the history of the earth. Each period has its own characteristic fossils, and the dates are arrived at by studying the breakdown of radioactive elements in volcanic and other igneous rocks.

As the Mesozoic drew to a close 65 million years ago, pterosaurs and theropods disappeared, leaving only birds to compete with mammals for dominance of the world. For a few million years, a quiet struggle took place for superiority on land, in the sea and in the air. In some places, birds became the dominant ground-dwelling carnivores and in some instances even became the largest ground-dwelling herbivores. Mammals also colonized the air, and both mammals and birds recolonized the sea. As mammals, we generally consider ourselves the dominant animals, but that is a self-centered attitude. The facts argue otherwise. Measured by species, birds outnumber mammals two to one, and in this sense it can easily be argued that dinosaurs, through their living descendants, are still more successful than mammals!

The Excitement of Discovery

My field of expertise is dinosaurs, and I have been involved in the excavation and study of many meat-eating species, including *Albertosaurus, Archaeornithomimus, Avimimus, Caenagnathus, Daspletosaurus, Oviraptor, Saurornitholestes, Troodon, Tyrannosaurus,* and several yet-to-be-named species from China. Finding and collecting dinosaurs is hard work by any standards. I have spent years searching for specimens in the badlands and deserts of North America and China. Once suitable specimens had been found, the work had only just begun, and it was anything but glamorous. Ahead were sometimes hundreds of hours spent painstakingly removing tons of rock. But when a good specimen is discovered, the rewards are instantaneous, and the excitement is hard to contain. Once, when photographing some badlands, I dropped my camera case down a hill. As I clambered down to retrieve it, you can imagine my surprise when I found it lying directly on a skull of *Daspletosaurus,* a smaller cousin of *Tyrannosaurus.* The specimen, which included most of the skeleton, had been entombed for 75 million years, and mine were the first human eyes to see it. Moments like this are exhilarating and yet deeply moving. Your breath is stopped for a moment when you realize this fossil is a window into the prehistoric world in which this animal fed and rested, had babies, bled and hurt like animals we know today.

Like my *Daspletosaurus* find, many of the best fossil discoveries are made entirely by chance. In 1979, I was part of a team completing the last of four expeditions to the Peace River Canyon in British Columbia. During these treks we had discovered more than 1,500 dinosaur footprints. As the final days closed on the expedition, we stopped for the last time at a familiar locality. We thought the area had given up all its secrets, but we were wrong. The river had unexpectedly risen overnight, and as the water fell away again, a rock layer split away to reveal more than 150 small footprints. I immediately realized that they were bird footprints, and because the rock was 120 million years old, they were one of the earliest records of fossil birds. Had we not made one last casual visit to that particular spot, these footprints and their message may have been lost to us forever.

Fossils that deepen our understanding of prehistoric life sometimes turn up in surprising places. As part of a Sino-Canadian expedition working near the northern Chinese city of Erenhot, I examined peculiar little hills of sand covered with fossil bones. These included the broken bones of an unusual and controversial little animal called *Avimimus*, which is classified as a bird by some scientists and as a dinosaur by others. But why should these bones appear on these little hills? It was an unsolvable mystery until we realized they were not ancient in origin. They had been left by bulldozers. Not knowing why bulldozers would be used so far from civilization, we made some inquiries and solved the mystery. In 1959, a joint Chinese and Russian expedition visiting the area had used bulldozers to strip the rock lying over a rich layer of bone. But in the process some bones had been bulldozed onto the piles. Over the years, much of the sand and mud had been removed by rain and wind, leaving a concentration of fossils on the surface. And here, in the rubble left by another fossil-hunting expedition, we discovered *Avimimus*.

A single fossil never provides a complete picture. Whenever you think you have discovered the largest dinosaur, an even larger one will be found. And when you think you have identified the most ancient flying vertebrate, you also could be in for a surprise. I remember the excitement at McGill University when my thesis supervisor, Dr. Robert L. Carroll, began his studies on the 250-million-year-old Permian reptiles of Madagascar. One type, a lizardlike coelurosauravid, had evolved very long ribs for supporting a gliding membrane. It seemed incredible that so soon after reptiles had originated, they had become diverse enough to dominate not only the land but had gone back to the sea and also conquered the air! I studied some of the Permian land-dwelling and swimming species from Madagascar, and Bob Carroll wrote an excellent study on these gliding reptiles.

Working with fossils is a lot like detective work. Evidence has to be examined, questions have to be answered and mysteries have to be solved. In 1856, Joseph Leidy described a tooth of *Troodon formosus*, which he thought belonged to a lizard. By the turn of the century, scientists realized it was really the tooth of a dinosaur, possibly a meat-eating species. Charles Gilmore agreed but identified it as the tooth of a plant-eating dome-headed dinosaur. Years later, two other palaeontologists published their opinions that Gilmore was wrong, and the tooth was again believed to be from a meat-eating dinosaur. By this time, several *Troodon* jaws had been found, although most of the teeth had been lost. Still, the remaining teeth clearly showed the jaws belonged to *Troodon* and the mystery about the 1856 tooth was solved. The story should have ended there in the 1940s, but it took a bizarre twist. First, one scientist continued to identify the teeth as *Troodon,* but identified the jaws as *Stenonychosaurus.* Another scientist put *Troodon* in one dinosaur family and *Stenonychosaurus* in another. Jack Horner entered the fray when he was studying these animals at his dinosaur egg site in Montana. He felt *Troodon* teeth were much like those of a plant-eating dinosaur called a hypsilophodont. Before he published his evidence, however, he discovered a new jaw close to where the Royal Tyrrell Museum of Palaeontology was being constructed in Drumheller, Alberta. The new specimen clearly showed that *Troodon* and *Stenonychosaurus* were the same animal and that it was a meat-eating dinosaur. The mystery of the tooth identified by Leidy was finally solved when I published my findings 130 years after his original description.

When fossils are discovered in the field, the initial identification of an interesting specimen sometimes proves to be very wrong. One evening, Dale Russell of the Canadian Museum of Nature came into our camp at Dinosaur Provincial Park in Alberta and reported he had discovered a dinosaur egg. We were eager to see it. While excavating the specimen the following day, we discovered it was not an egg, but something just as remarkable. A long pterosaur bone had been sectioned by erosion so only a cross-section of the shaft was exposed at the surface. The diameter of the shaft was about six centimeters, but the bone surrounding the hollow space was less than two millimeters thick, which is close to the thickness of a dinosaur eggshell. The bone really did look like an egg until enough rock was removed to expose the shaft. Dale Russell had found the very first record of the giant pterosaur *Quetzalcoatlus* in Canada.

Palaeontology is often the science of recognizing big discoveries in small things. To be important, specimens do not have to be big or pretty or complete. In 1986, a Chinese palaeontologist working with our crews in Dinosaur Provincial Park discovered the back of the skull of the human-sized dinosaur *Troodon*. The specimen was no larger than a man's fist. But during the millions of years it lay buried, it had not been crushed and was still riddled with holes for nerves, blood-vessels and air pockets. Here was evidence of birdlike characteristics we did not expect at the time to find in any dinosaur, and this tiny fossil helped us understand how birds could have arisen from dinosaurs.

Our effort to understand one of the great mysteries of Earth history – the origin of flight – has been filled with such chance discoveries, surprising twists, mysteries, misidentifications and rediscoveries. They are all part of the excitement of discovery.

The
Evolution of Flight

ICHTHYORNIS

*F*or many people, flight is as incomprehensible as the idea of geological time. Imagining the distant reaches of Earth history is as difficult as conceiving of air having enough resistance to hold up an animal's body, let alone an enormous jumbo jet. Although we cannot see it, air is a thin fluid animals use for locomotion. It does not exert much pressure when we walk or run through it, but we need only think of the devastating power of hurricanes, typhoons and tornadoes to realize how much resistance it can exert on us. If you try to drag a parachute or large kite, you also become aware of its force. By increasing the surface area of its body or alternately reducing its weight while staying the same size, an animal can increase its ability to use air as a fluid to "swim" through.

For the purposes of this book, I identify three levels of flight – gliding (including parachuting), active flying and soaring. Gliding and parachuting slow the rate of descent by increasing the body's surface areas to increase resistance to the air. Under the right circumstances, efficient gliders can travel great distances, but they often have to climb to a high point before initiating a gliding action and generally cannot move effectively against strong air movements like prevailing winds. Gliders are never completely masters of the air.

Specialized membranes allow many animals to glide short distances.

To achieve active flight, an animal needs more power to gain greater control of its movements. Humans engineered active flight through the use of winged machines powered by jet engines or propellers, but birds, bats and pterosaurs accomplished this extraordinary evolutionary feat through the use of muscular power alone.

The third level of flight, soaring, should be possible for efficient gliders that take advantage of air movements like thermals or updrafts to carry them aloft. This is how a kite becomes airborne. Yet in nature, soaring has generally been restricted to large pterosaurs and birds, and these flap their wings only to gain the altitude necessary to take advantage of thermals and updrafts. This suggests that these animals sacrificed active flight to become larger. Bats, for example, never became as large as the bigger pterosaurs and birds, and so have never become soaring animals.

Like animals, plants have found ways to use air currents to carry pollen, spores and seeds great distances. The parachutelike extension of the dandelion seed (left) is common among plants, but the helicopterlike wing of a maple key (right) is unique.

Over time, both plants and animals have taken advantage of the resistant properties of air. Among plants are thousands of species that use moving air to disperse tiny spores or pollen, or to carry larger seeds on "wings" or "parachutes." Although these mechanisms can carry reproductive plant matter for hundreds of kilometers, plants do not have powered flight, and their seeds must follow the whims of the air currents (unless of course they hitch a ride on a flying animal).

Life forms have always been quick to exploit new frontiers. Plants and animals originated in the seas but had moved onto the land by the Devonian Period, 395 – 345 million years ago. And before the period closed, plants were using air currents to disperse spores, and shortly after insects had evolved wings and taken to the air. The thin envelope of atmosphere surrounding our planet was conquered 350 million years before human beings looked enviously at creatures of the air and their freedom to fly.

Why Fly?

The Arctic tern is a champion flier, migrating from pole to pole each year.

Flight offers many advantages for plants and animals. Dispersal by air is important to both because it increases the distances that can be traveled and provides opportunities to colonize new areas that may not be accessible by land or sea. Flight also decreases the amount of energy and time required to move any distance. The Arctic tern, for example, could not complete its annual 30000-kilometer migration between the Arctic and Antarctic if it had to walk! For other animals, flight is a way of escaping predators. And for still others, it is a way to find and capture prey. Greg Paul, author of *Predatory Dinosaurs of the World,* makes the case that flight is actually less complicated than walking, so it should be no surprise that it has been adopted by so many different types of animals.

The Last Frontier
ANIMALS CONQUER THE SKY

Insects were probably the first animals to master powered flight. The fossil record clearly shows that 350 million years ago, insects had already evolved wings. And what wings! Imagine a dragonfly with a wingspan of close to a meter! But insects are not the only invertebrates (animals without backbones) capable of flying. A startling example is the flying squid, which can launch itself up to five meters out of the water.

Every major group of vertebrates (animals with backbones) has taken advantage of some form of flight, whether it be gliding, active flying or soaring. Flying fish of the family Exocoetidae have greatly enlarged front fins (in some forms extending all the way back to the tail) that allow them to glide through the air. Their large tail fins are adapted for getting them up to high speeds so they can leave the water with enough momentum to carry them any distance. A half-meter-long fish can stay aloft for a dozen or so seconds and can cover as much as 200 meters at speeds of up to 50 kilometers per hour.

Flying frogs (*Rhacophorus reinwardii*) of the Sunda Islands flatten their bodies and spread their large toes so the webs can act as gliding membranes. Because their toes are not as long as the fingers of bats or pterosaurs, flying frogs are limited to gliding only a few meters between plants.

Lizards have evolved flight in more than one lineage. The flying gecko (*Platydactylus homalocephalus*) has a fold of skin along the sides of its body and tail, a membrane between its wrist and shoulder, and webbing between its toes. These allow it to glide short distances. *Draco*, the flying dragon from southeast Asia, is perhaps the most successful modern lizard of the air. Its five or six pairs of ribs extend sideways well beyond the normal body line to support a skin membrane. The ribs are flexible, giving the animal some maneuverability as it glides from tree to tree. Although the flying dragon is seldom airborne for more than 15 meters, it can gain elevation by taking advantage of updrafts.

Flying fish escape predators by leaving the water at high speed and gliding through the air for as much as 200 meters before reentering the water.

Flying frogs open their toes to produce four parachutes when they leap from plant to plant. The parachutes create drag, slowing their descent.

The gliding membrane of Draco *is supported by its ribs, which fold back alongside the body when the lizard is at rest.*

Reptiles and mammals exhibit many types of gliding membranes. The parachuting gecko (1) uses the frills along the sides of its head, body and tail, and spreads out its webbed toes. Flying squirrels (2) and lemurs (3) have membranes that stretch when they extend their legs out from their bodies. The flying snake (4) simply flattens its body to increase its resistance to the air.

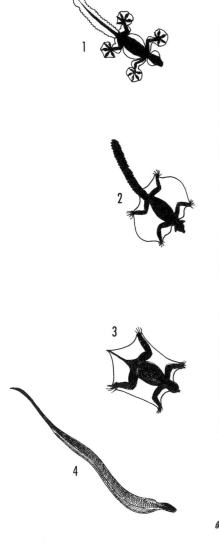

Snakes seem unlikely candidates for flight, but there is actually a flying snake *(Chrysopelea ornata)* in southeast Asia, India and Sri Lanka. This snake climbs trees, and when it wants to move to another branch or tree, it coils its body like a spring and launches into the air. By flattening its body to increase air resistance against its fall, it can glide short distances.

Among airborne mammals are several marsupials, including species of flying phalangers. One species, *Petaurus norfolcensis*, from Australia, Tasmania and New Guinea, uses a membrane between its front and hind limbs as a sail and its tail as a rudder. It can glide up to 55 meters. The Greater Gliding Possum *(Schoinobates rolans)* is a larger mammal (up to a meter long if you include the tail) that can glide up to 100 meters between trees.

Several lineages of more progressive placental mammals have also taken to the air. Two species of the flying lemur *Cynocephalus*, belonging to the mammalian order Dermoptera, have a large muscular membrane extending from the neck to the front leg, from the wrist to the ankle and from the hind leg to the end of the tail. These animals are thought to be more closely related to primates and bats than to any other living mammals. Although the fossil record of dermopterans is scanty, a closely related group, the Plagiomenidae, was widespread in North America some 55 million years ago and may provide clues to the evolution of dermopteran flight. Flying lemurs move awkwardly on the ground and so spend most of their time in trees. These gliders lose as little as 15 meters of elevation during a 100-meter glide.

Flying squirrels are successful rodents whose gliding membranes stretch from their wrists to their ankles. Although seldom seen because they are active only at night, two species inhabit North America and another dozen genera are found in Asia. These mammals usually glide for only short distances, enough to move between trees. Yet an Asian squirrel was once observed gliding almost half a kilometer in a strong updraft.

Bats, the only actively flying mammals, have a long fossil record, stretching back almost 60 million years. The two main lineages of bats, the fruit-eating megachiropterans and insect-eating microchiropterans, both have wing membranes supported by four greatly elongated fingers. In contrast, the flying reptiles have only one finger supporting the wing. Birds have reduced the length of the wing fingers, leaving the function of support to their feathers.

The first true flying reptiles, the pterosaurs, had appeared by the end of the Triassic, 213 million years ago. Some palaeontologists feel they evolved from a group of fossil reptiles that also gave rise to the dinosaurs. It was once even proposed that pterosaurs were the descendants of carnivorous dinosaurs.

The earliest undisputed record of birds dates from 70 million years later and consists of six *Archaeopteryx* skeletons from the Late Jurassic. However, skeletons found in 1986 in 225 million-year-old rocks in Texas suggest birds may have originated about the same time as pterosaurs.

Flying vertebrates of all kinds tend to share many characteristics evolved in response to the requirements of flight. For example, all active fliers – pterosaurs, birds and bats – have hollow bones to reduce their body weight and some fused joints between bones to reduce the flexibility of their bodies for more precise but fewer movements. Because active flying requires constant high levels of energy, pterosaurs, birds and bats all became warm-blooded.

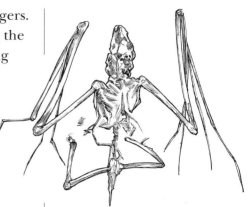

Well-preserved fossils from North America and Europe show that bats perfected their mode of flight in the Eocene. They have changed very little over the past 50 million years.

Big-eared bats of the northern hemisphere are typical microchiropterans. Most eat insects, located by a form of radar known as echolocation. Radar has largely replaced sight in this nocturnal hunter.

Fruit bats, which are larger than insect-eating bats, have wings supported by four enormously elongated fingers. The small thumb is free from the wing and ends in a claw.

The Rarity of Fliers in the Fossil Record

The study of prehistoric flying animals is difficult because their remains are generally rare. Only a tiny fraction of animals perish in conditions ideal for fossilization. Bodies must be buried before they are destroyed by scavengers, decomposition and weathering. Even if they are buried in mud or shifting sand before predation, the groundwater may be too acidic, and the bones may dissolve underground. And then the covering of mud or sand may be washed or blown away again before the process of fossilization is complete.

The chance of flying animals being fossilized is even smaller. Most live and hunt over land, and when they die, their bodies fall to the ground where they are either eaten by scavengers or decomposed by bacteria. Because they are lightly built, their bones are fragile and easily destroyed. The hollow bones of birds and pterosaurs, for example, are like tubes, the walls of which are seldom more than a few millimeters thick.

Coelurosauravus (top), Kuehneosaurus (middle) and Draco (bottom) look similar because of their rib-supported gliding membranes. Yet they are not closely related, and each evolved independently from non-gliding forms. This is a classic example of convergence, or the evolution of similar characters in animals not ancestrally related to each other.

Our knowledge of the evolution of flying animals is restricted to a few key areas where, as we will see, conditions for fossilization were ideal. The lithographic limestones of Solnhofen, Germany, is one. The chalks of Kansas is another. All were at one time marine environments, and while rich in fossil remains, even they may not give an accurate picture of the diversity of flying animals that lived over the land.

Despite the scantiness of the fossil record, scientists have determined that reptiles first took to the air 250 million years ago with bizarre gliding forms known as coelurosauravids. Looking much like modern flying lizards, their gliding membranes were supported by very long ribs. But coelurosauravids were only distantly related to their relatives, the lizards. Their body form was obviously a good one for gliding because it appears twice in the fossil record, the second time in a primitive group of lizards known as kuehneosaurids. One example, *Icarosaurus*, was a form that lived in North America more than 200 million years ago.

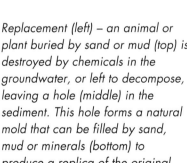

Permineralization (right) – quartz or other minerals carried by groundwater fill small pores and holes in bones or plant material. Most dinosaur bones are permineralized.

Carbonization (above) – the organic parts of a plant or animal break down, leaving only a carbon trace in the rock.

Fossils are the evidence used by palaeontologists (scientists who study ancient life) to identify animals and plants living before us and to understand how they lived. Many people think fossilization means something is "turned to stone," or petrified. But this is not necessarily the case. For example, the wood of 100-million-year-old logs found near Fort McMurray, Alberta, has changed very little since the trees died. The logs have simply been pickled in the oils of the tar sands found there. Other types of fossilization include replacement, permineralization, carbonization and impression.

Replacement (left) – an animal or plant buried by sand or mud (top) is destroyed by chemicals in the groundwater, or left to decompose, leaving a hole (middle) in the sediment. This hole forms a natural mold that can be filled by sand, mud or minerals (bottom) to produce a replica of the original.

Impression (left) – an animal stepping or lying in mud (top) can leave an impression (middle) of what its foot or skin looked like, though the animal did not die and leave its bones. Later, sediment fills the impression (bottom).

COELUROSAURAVUS
A Gliding Reptile of the Permian

When reptiles first appeared, they adapted quickly to a variety of lifestyles on the land, in the sea and even in the air. *Coelurosauravus*, appearing about 250 million years ago on the island of Madagascar, is the earliest known gliding reptile. Its ribs extended far beyond its body outline to support a gliding membrane. A close relative, *Weigeltisaurus*, lived in Europe around the same time, suggesting coelurosauravids were widespread and quite successful. *Coelurosauravus* has several features in common with modern lizards. Its skull is reminiscent of a chameleon's, and its rib-supported gliding membrane was similar to that of *Draco*.

As *COELUROSAURAVUS* GLIDES ACROSS A pool in a primeval Madagascar forest, it is too intent on capturing its prey to notice the imminent danger of a larger reptile, *Hovasaurus*, breaking the water's surface from below. In the branch of a tree overhead, a silent witness, *Acerosodontosaurus*, awaits the outcome.

The **P**terosaurs
THE DRAGONS OF THE AIR

SCLEROMOCHLUS

The History of Pterosaur Discovery

The first pterosaur discovery was reported in 1784 by Cosimo Collini, a former secretary to French philosopher and writer Voltaire. The specimen was found in the lithographic limestones of Solnhofen, Germany. By a rare coincidence of natural occurrences, the Solnhofen limestone formations have become one of the world's greatest storehouses of marine animal, flying reptile and early bird fossils. Here, 140 million years ago, life thrived in a tropical lagoon nestled behind a barrier reef in a sea that covered much of central Europe. Conditions for fossilization were ideal. The lagoon's hypersalinity discouraged scavengers from destroying carcasses. As they settled to the lagoon's bottom, they were covered with fine sediments that later turned to stone. In this natural tomb, creatures were preserved in exquisite detail and lay undisturbed until the Romans began to quarry this prized building material 2000 years ago. Later, these fine-grained slabs, which polish to the sheen of marble, were discovered to be ideal for making plates for the printing process called lithography. As workers laboriously split the stone by hand into thin sheets, they inevitably began to discover clues to the region's ancient past. Throughout the years, the Solnhofen quarries have produced thousands of fossils, including many species of pterosaurs and the earliest known bird, *Archaeopteryx*.

Collini's remarkable find was not originally classified as a flying animal. He thought the pterosaur's winglike structure propelled it through the water. The great French anatomist Cuvier later recognized the remains as those of a flying animal, but his interpretation went unnoticed by some. In 1830, the German zoologist Johann Wagler linked pterosaurs to marine reptiles, considering them intermediate between mammals and birds, and reconstructed one as a swimming creature with penguinlike wings and rudder-shaped feet.

The first pterosaur fossil came from the limestone quarries of Germany's Solnhofen region in 1784. From this rich fossil repository, palaeontologists have recovered many remarkably complete skeletons.

Pterosaur remains continue to be found in Germany's lithographic limestones. Many well-preserved specimens are complete skeletons, and some even have skin impressions revealing the structure of the wing membranes. To date, they have revealed more about pterosaur anatomy and lifestyles than specimens from any other region of the world.

Because flying animals have tremendous mobility, it is not surprising that pterosaur remains have also been collected in recent years from every continent except Antarctica, and it is only a matter of time before they are found there too. After all, people did not expect to find dinosaurs on the island continent at the South Pole, but at least three dinosaur skeletons have been collected there since 1986. If dinosaurs lived and died there, we can bet pterosaurs did too. During the prehistoric time of the pterosaur, the Antarctic climate was much warmer than today, even when locked in the unrelenting darkness of the long polar winters.

During the early part of the nineteenth century, pterosaurs were recovered from the mudstones and chalks of southern England. Thousands of isolated bones have been recovered from the Greensand deposits near Oxford and from the famous white cliffs near Dover. Although generally not as well preserved as the German fossils, most English specimens represent different species, some of which are pterosaurs as large as those collected in the United States.

As the American West was settled during the mid-nineteenth century, fossil hunting parties also started to recover well-preserved skeletons of enormous flying reptiles from the chalk deposits of western Kansas. The famous fossil wars of Othniel Charles Marsh of New Haven and Edward Drinker Cope of Philadelphia set the tone of the era as these men poured their personal wealth into competing for the collection and description of as many fossils as possible. Crews working for Marsh were particularly successful, and many of these specimens reside today in the collections of Yale University's Peabody Museum of Natural History. *Pteranodon*, then widely publicized as the largest flying animal, remains the most famous and one of the best understood of Marsh's discoveries.

In 1972, the remains of a gigantic pterosaur, with an estimated wingspan of 12 meters, were found at Big Bend National Park in Texas. The "Ptexas Pterosaur," better known as *Quetzalcoatlus*, was considerably larger than the previous record holder, *Pteranodon*, whose wings spanned only eight meters. The *Quetzalcoatlus* discovery brought public attention to these fascinating flying reptiles again. It came at a time of increased levels of scientific investigation of pterosaurs, research that remains active to this day. This research encompasses describing pterosaur anatomy and new species, studying how they flew, how their bodies functioned, how they behaved and even how they were related to other animals.

Most pterosaur remains found around the world are poorly preserved fragments, but they are still distinctive enough for identification. In Alberta, up to a dozen pterosaur bones are recovered every year, although no complete skeleton has yet been found.

Compared with Quetzalcoatlus, the average person is dwarfed. The largest known flying animal, Quetzalcoatlus had the wingspan of a twin-engine aircraft.

What is a Pterosaur?

The word *pterosaur* means "wing lizard," although these animals are better known to English-speaking people as flying reptiles. Pterosaurs appeared in the fossil record around the same time as dinosaurs and mammals, and disappeared with the dinosaurs at the end of the Mesozoic Era, 65 million years ago. Although they died without leaving descendants, pterosaurs survived for 140 million years, reason enough to judge them very successful creatures.

The most obvious characteristic of pterosaurs was their leathery batlike wings, each supported by a greatly elongated index finger. The joint at the base of the wing finger was specialized so the wing could be folded next to the body when not in use. Flying reptiles had four joints in their wing-supporting finger, one less than found in a normal reptilian index finger. Because a claw at the end of the wing was not needed, the claw-bearing bone was probably the segment lost. Pterosaurs' first three fingers, equivalent to our

Bird, pterosaur and fruit bat wings have many similarities. The bird's fingers (top) have fused, while one finger in the pterosaur (middle) and four in the bat (bottom) have elongated to support the wing membranes. This transformation of arms into wings is an example of convergent evolution, but clearly the wings of these three animals have evolved in very different ways.

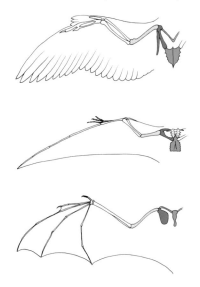

thumb and next two fingers, were free for grasping prey, branches, rocks and whatever else a normal hand is needed for. These three free fingers all bore narrow but deep claws, which were relatively long and sharp. The fifth, or "little," finger, normally found in the reptilian hand, was lost. A new bone, called the pteroid, appeared on the front of the hand. It stiffened the leading edge of a membrane extending from the wrist to the base of the neck. Among the reptiles, pterosaurs had the most highly adapted hands.

Wings are not the only peculiarity of pterosaurs. Their unusually large skulls can be anywhere from 50 to 90 percent of the torso's length. Although enormous, the skull is always very light and airy, with large openings in the bone between the nostril and the eye. The purpose of these openings, also found in dinosaurs and birds, is uncertain, but they may have evolved to reduce the weight of the head.

The brains of most land animals are surrounded by skull bones, and we can learn much about the brains of extinct animals by studying casts of hollowed-out braincases. Such laboratory studies conducted on pterosaur skulls reveal that their brains were relatively large and birdlike. Pterosaurs had good vision, a high level of muscular coordination, but a poor sense of smell. Pterosaurs may have been as intelligent as some birds, but the relationship between brain size and intelligence is not clear. Some scientists think large brain size may be an indicator of body temperature rather than intelligence. For example, many animals with small brains have complex behaviors normally attributed only to highly intelligent animals. Pterosaurs' large brain size also may confirm they were warm-blooded. Among modern animals, the only vertebrates with large brains are warm-blooded birds and mammals.

The front bones of pterosaurs' upper jaws are fused, and even in forms retaining teeth, a horny bill seems to have been present at the front of the jaws. The sharp bill was probably used to break the surface of the water quickly and cleanly when pterosaurs thrust their jaws into the water to catch fish. Teeth, when present, are sharp, curved, flattened from side to side and without serrations along the cutting edges. Pterosaur teeth were suitable for capturing and killing, but not for tearing or cutting meat.

The pterosaur shoulder girdle is very birdlike, which is not surprising, because they used their wings in much the same way as birds. The shoulder blade is straplike, and the breastbone is a large plate for bracing the wings and anchoring the massive flight muscles. Unlike birds and some dinosaurs, pterosaurs did not have a wishbone. The upper arm bone is distinctive because of a huge leverlike crest that the flight muscles attached to.

As in most mammals, the pterosaur backbone can be divided into distinct neck, thoracic, lumbar, sacral and tail sections. Although the length of the neck can vary tremendously, the number of vertebrae is, interestingly, always seven. Many pterosaurs had long graceful necks, possibly to allow them to fish with quick lunging motions as they glided low over the water. The pterosaur's long neck also may have helped it distribute the weight of its large head more evenly by carrying it back over its shoulders. The vertebrae at the front of the body are hollow and connected to the lungs by pneumatic tubes. This peculiar characteristic, also found in birds and saurischian dinosaurs, reduces body weight by allowing air into the bones. The pneumatic tubes may serve as a cooling system and oxygen reserve in warm-blooded animals. Air pockets from the lungs also invaded many of the pterosaur's arm and leg bones, which have extremely thin but dense walls, again in a way similar to birds.

The upper leg bone has a distinct ball-like head offset from the shaft. This bone and its relationship to the hips have been analyzed extensively in recent years to determine if pterosaurs had an efficient upright stride or a sprawling clumsy gait. One theory, which dominated for many years, maintained that pterosaurs were incapable of walking upright. However, pterosaurs tended to have long legs, and when the hip, leg and foot bones are articulated, it appears likely at least some pterosaurs walked and ran upright like dinosaurs, birds and mammals. The shin bone is sometimes double the length of the upper leg bone, suggesting some pterosaurs were swift and agile runners. Generally, the foot has five toes. The outermost toe is usually long, but diverges from the other toes in a manner similar to our thumbs. Many artists have incorrectly shown this toe supporting the lower edge of a web of skin between the back legs. This membrane is present in bats and in at least some pterosaurs, but this pterosaur toe is on the wrong side of the foot

Birds (left), pterosaurs (middle) and bats (right) are similar in that the bones of the chest strongly brace the shoulders. Bird and pterosaur breastbones are especially large and platelike for the attachment of flight muscles.

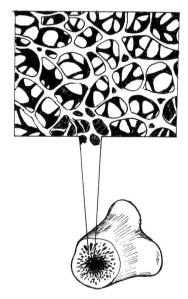

Pterosaur and bird bones are hollow and often filled with air to make them lightweight. Near the ends of the limb bones, thin filaments span the air space to add strength where needed.

to support it. More probably, the pterosaur's outer toe helped it grasp things.

What we know about the soft anatomy of pterosaurs comes from some remarkably well-preserved fossils. The wing membrane of a Brazilian pterosaur, probably *Santanadactylus*, is so well preserved that the layers of skin can be studied. Several specimens of *Rhamphorhynchus* and *Pterodactylus* collected in Germany show exquisitely detailed wing membranes. The wing membrane is reinforced internally by long thin fibers stiffening the outer part of the wing and stopping the trailing edge from fluttering, which would have caused air turbulence and reduced the wing's ability to create lift. The fibers are arched to give the wing the aerodynamically efficient shape also seen in the wings of birds and airplanes. A tendon extends along the leading edge of the wing membrane between the front of the arm and the base of the neck. The tension on this tendon was controlled by arm muscles, probably allowing pterosaurs to adjust the camber of their wings during flight. Other fossils indicate the possibility of other remarkable adaptations. A *Scaphognathus* specimen from Bonn, Germany, has small tubular structures on parts of the wing. They look much like the quills of undeveloped feathers. A more remarkable specimen, *Sordes*, found in Kazakhstan in central Asia, appears to be covered by fur.

Epidermis

Dermis

Crystals formed during fossilization

Muscle fibers

The wing membrane of a Brazilian pterosaur is composed of several layers. The outer layer, the epidermis, has a rippled pattern similar to human skin. The next two layers form the dermis, through which passes a network of capillary veins. The lowermost layer is made up of muscle fibers. In this specimen, crystals formed during fossilization separated the skin from the muscle fibers.

The Origin of Pterosaurs

Our understanding of the origin of flying reptiles is intimately linked to our knowledge of the animals most closely related to pterosaurs. When pterosaurs appeared in the fossil record, they were already highly specialized flying animals. And during their 140-million-year reign, they changed very little. No "missing link" like *Archaeopteryx*, the evolutionary bridge between dinosaurs and birds, exists, making pterosaur origins more open to speculation.

In his 1983 study of the early pterosaur *Preondactylus*, Rupert Wild suggested flying reptiles may have evolved directly from a primitive reptile group that also gave rise to lizards, plesiosaurs (large marine reptiles) and the common ancestors of crocodiles and dinosaurs. Wild found that these animals had much in common. He based his conclusion on similarities in the skull, hands and feet, and the presence of a bony breastbone, an opposable outer toe, more than one cusp on the teeth and the way the teeth are implanted.

Almost a century ago, the English palaeontologist Harry Govier Seeley argued in favor of a close relationship between pterosaurs, birds and dinosaurs, which have many comparable features in the skull, brain, leg and ankle. Seeley was especially impressed by the invasion of air sacs from the lungs into these animals' vertebrae.

Most palaeontologists now believe pterosaurs evolved from the dinosaur's immediate ancestors, including such dinosaurlike reptiles as *Lagosuchus* from Argentina and *Scleromochlus* from Scotland. Friedrich von Huene studied the half dozen *Scleromochlus taylori* skeletons in 1914 and concluded that this 220-million-year-old animal was close to the origin of flying reptiles. Although *Scleromochlus* was not a flying or gliding animal, it had many characteristics also found in pterosaurs. The skull is very large compared with the body, and its large openings give it a lightweight appearance. Its strap-shaped shoulder blade can be compared to either a pterosaur's or a dinosaur's. The backbone is divided into neck, thoracic, lumbar, pelvic and tail regions. *Scleromochlus* probably ran on hind legs held under its body, a dramatic departure from the sprawling gait of many reptiles. The lower leg bones are long, as are the bones in the flat of the foot. When Kevin Padian restudied the *Scleromochlus* specimens 70 years after von Huene's original examination, he found additional characters in the ankle to support the relationship of *Scleromochlus* to flying reptiles.

Most palaeontologists accept that pterosaurs originated from *Scleromochlus* or one of its close relatives. At one time *Scleromochlus* would have been called an advanced thecodont, one of a hodgepodge animal group including the common ancestors of crocodiles, phytosaurs, dinosaurs and pterosaurs. But today, scientists recognize that its specializations make it at least close to the ancestor of both pterosaurs and dinosaurs. In fact, some scientists consider it a small dinosaur.

SCLEROMOCHLUS TAYLORI
An Ancestor of the Dinosaurs and Pterosaurs?

The English palaeontologist A. Smith-Woodward described *Scleromochlus* in 1907 from specimens collected from Upper Triassic rocks near Elgin, Scotland. The specimens were reexamined by the famous German palaeontologist Friedrich von Huene, who published his observations seven years later. He speculated that *Scleromochlus* may have climbed high in trees and may even have had gliding membranes to help it leap from one location to another. Not all scientists accept this interpretation. Some feel *Scleromochlus* was better adapted for jumping and hopping like a kangaroo rat. Recent geological studies tend to prove the second interpretation correct because few, if any, trees existed at Elgin 220 million years ago. The region was a desert.

Scleromochlus was only 20 centimeters in total length, most of it made up of its large head and very long tail. Although this peculiar little animal may not have been the direct forerunner of pterosaurs, von Huene and many subsequent researchers think it may be closely related to the true pterosaur ancestor.

A PAIR OF TINY *Scleromochlus,* competing for prey in the harsh environment of prehistoric Scotland, had little inclination to ponder their future. But they did have a future in that their descendants may have been the winged pterosaurs.

Pterosaur Flight

Pterosaurs were the first active fliers among the vertebrates. They had all the adaptations necessary for flapping flight that birds and bats have, but few of the specializations seen in gliding animals. Pterosaurs, birds and bats have specialized joints in their arms for moving them in powerful down-and-forward strokes. The pterosaur's broad breastbone, with its pronounced keel, and the large process on its upper arm bone indicate it had much more powerful flight muscles than needed in a gliding animal. The strongly braced shoulder girdle is another indication of strong flight strokes. Undoubtedly, all but the largest pterosaurs were efficient active fliers that could cover great distances. The largest pterosaurs, like the largest birds, developed techniques for soaring and would have flapped their wings only to gain altitude, change direction or increase their speed.

The origin of pterosaur flight has inspired much speculation. Some scientists believe pterosaurs began as tree-climbing reptiles that evolved long arms and gliding membranes to swoop from tree to tree. Friedrich von Huene envisioned *Scleromochlus* as the first step in this series, but as we have seen, evidence suggests this animal lived in a desert and was not therefore a tree-climber. While all pterosaurs had hands with large sharp claws suitable for climbing trees, the claws on the hind feet were smaller and less sharp. If pterosaurs were tree-climbers, we would expect the claws of both front and hind limbs to be equally sharp.

Study of the sturdy hind legs of Dimorphodon *has convinced palaeontologists that many flying reptiles could walk and run upright. This suggests they evolved from ground-dwelling animals. As in all pterosaurs, the skull of* Dimorphodon *was disproportionately large. However, large sinuses kept the skull very light, and it was counterbalanced by the tail.*

Other scientists argue that pterosaur fossils provide no evidence for a tree-dwelling way of life, but that flying reptiles were well adapted for running on the ground. Pterosaurs had long legs, walked on the ends of their toes (as do dogs and cats, but not bears or people), and had hip, knee and foot joints similar to those of upright animals like birds. If early pterosaurs had stronger adaptations for running on the ground than for living in trees, then it is more likely pterosaur flight originated from the ground up than from the trees down.

At one time, palaeontologists thought pterosaurs were not efficient fliers. If they were to become airborne, the reasoning went, they would have to climb trees or high cliffs. A single wing finger was judged to provide less effective support for the wing membrane than the four fingers supporting the wing of a bat. But we now know that the pterosaur wing was braced for stability and had an efficient aerodynamic shape. The need for pterosaurs to glide from higher altitudes now seems unlikely. As we have seen, their limbs were not adapted for climbing, and species that fished or swam far out at sea had to have the power to take off directly from the water's surface. Wind tunnel studies of *Pteranodon* models suggest that a 17-kilogram animal with a seven-meter wingspan would have risen rapidly in an updraft and would have experienced only a slight tendency to lose altitude when soaring. *Pteranodon* was probably a slow but maneuverable flier. With a lower stall speed than birds, it would have landed softly on its legs.

Pterosaur wings actually bore less weight than those of similarly sized birds. Later forms without tails would have had less horizontal stability than tailed pterosaurs and birds, but they would have changed direction more rapidly. Such high maneuverability suggests very sophisticated muscle coordination by a relatively advanced brain.

Pterosaur Lifestyles

The first flying reptiles of the Late Triassic lived in a world much different than the one we know today. Windswept deserts dominated what is now North and South America, while Africa and Europe were largely covered by lush vegetation. But the last pterosaurs shared the earth with many plants and animals that have relatives alive today. By Cretaceous times, flowering plants and conifers had become dominant, and animals like garfish, sturgeons, soft-shelled turtles, crocodiles, alligators, shorebirds and opossumlike mammals were common.

The skull of Tropeognathus has many closely packed teeth in the long lower jaws. This pterosaur's teeth acted like a sieve to strain small invertebrates from seawater.

Fish scales and bones found in the rib cages of several pterosaur fossils suggest many species were fish-eaters. These meals had not been digested when the animals perished and were fossilized.

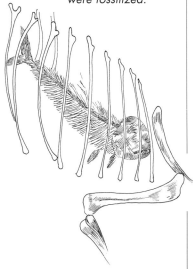

Pterosaurs, like modern birds, were highly diverse and adapted to a variety of lifestyles. Like most birds, but unlike bats, they were active by the day and roosted by night. Flying reptiles came in many shapes and sizes, and inhabited a wide range of environments. Some lived on land, some along ancient coastlines and some hunted hundreds of kilometers out to sea. But with few exceptions, known pterosaurs seem to have filled the ecological niche occupied today by shorebirds. Pterosaurs were egg-laying animals, and some lived in colonies to protect their hatchlings, suggesting that at least some may have been very caring parents.

Most pterosaur teeth and jaws were ideal for either an insect- or fish-eating lifestyle. Fossilized stomach contents confirm that several species ate fish, and it is safe to assume that most other known flying reptiles were fish-eaters too. Fish fossils also have been found in an impression of a pterosaur's throat sac, so at least some species evolved a pouch, similar to a pelican's, in which to store food. Other pterosaurs had many thin but closely packed teeth for straining tiny invertebrates from water. Many later flying reptiles lacked teeth, which may indicate they developed lifestyles like vultures, scavenging the carcasses of dinosaurs.

The flying reptiles' body contours were not designed for efficient swimming, so they probably skimmed just above the water and caught fish moving near the surface. Some pterosaurs, however, may have dived into the water from higher altitudes, just as some modern birds do. Well-preserved specimens show that at least some pterosaurs had webbed feet, an obvious adaptation for swimming.

Pterosaur Diversity

More than 90 species of pterosaurs have been discovered. This number is not large, considering they survived so long over so much of the earth. By comparison, birds have evolved into over

8000 species. Probably thousands of pterosaur species with special adaptations for many different environments remain to be discovered. Almost 20 percent of known species come from the 140-million-year-old lithographic limestones at Solnhofen in central Germany. Conditions for fossilization at Solnhofen were superb not only for the preservation of flying reptiles, but also for fish, lizards, dinosaurs and birds. The abundance of fossils produced by these rare conditions gives us an idea of how rich and diverse life may have been at any one time in any one region of the world.

Since most pterosaur fossils are found in sediments deposited under ancient seas, it seems reasonable to conclude that the great majority were sea-going, fish-eating animals. But this interpretation is probably misleading for two reasons. First, pterosaurs may have

The Pterosauria includes more than 90 distinct species, some of which are represented on this family tree. They are divided into two major groups, the Rhamphorhynchoidea and the Pterodactyloidea.

Pterosaur Family Tree

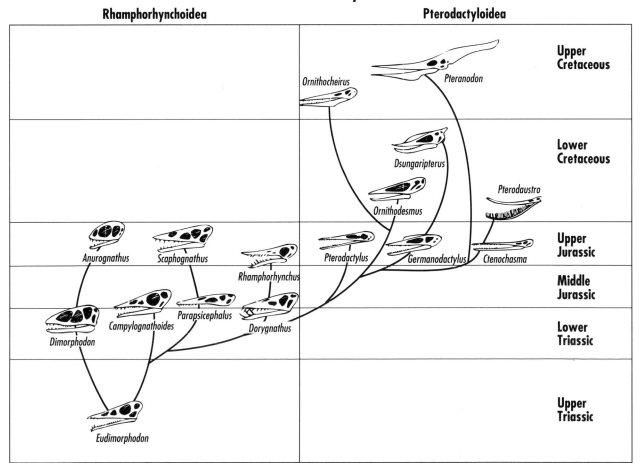

This rhamphorhynchoid skeleton, seen from above, shows the characteristic

short wrist bones, long outermost toe and long tail of the species.

This pterodactyloid skeleton, seen from below,
shows its advanced features – a long skull and neck, a short tail, long wrist bones and short outermost toes. The pterodactyloid model was faster and more maneuverable but less stable aero-dynamically. The pterodactyl's larger brain likely compensated for the instability.

existed with great diversity over the land where conditions for the preservation of skeletons were not ideal. And secondly, some pterosaurs found in marine rocks may have been blown or washed out to sea. The fossil records of other regions may yet disclose as rich a record as is found at Solnhofen.

Pterosaurs are divided into two major lineages, the Rhamphorhynchoidea and the Pterodactyloidea. The primitive rhamphorhynchoids dominated the air during the Triassic and Jurassic Periods. The more advanced pterodactyloid pterosaurs, or simply pterodactyls, first appeared in the Late Jurassic and later ruled the Cretaceous skies. Compared with rhamphorhynchoids, pterodactyls have longer skulls and necks, fused backbones in the shoulder region, longer wrist bones, and shorter tails and fifth toes. These anatomical refinements made the pterodactyls faster and more maneuverable fliers. Some pterodactyls also sported large and unusual head crests.

Pterosaur Extinction

After successfully occupying the skies for more than 140 million years, pterosaurs perished with the last dinosaurs 65 million years ago. Nobody knows why pterosaurs, dinosaurs and many other animals died out at the end of the Cretaceous. Much controversy surrounds this period of high extinction, but not enough evidence is available to answer even the most basic questions. How much time was involved in the great period of dying? We do not know, but the flying reptiles seem to have been declining in diversity over millions of years, which means extinction did not occur at a catastrophic rate. Perhaps pterosaurs were gradually driven to extinction by birds, which had become progressively more diverse and dominant throughout the Cretaceous. Did the decline of the pterosaurs occur around the world simultaneously? Again, we have no answer.

Most dinosaur extinction theories are relevant to the final disappearance of flying reptiles in the fossil record. A popular recent explanation suggests an asteroid struck the earth with great velocity 65 million years ago. Such an event would throw a tremendous volume of dust into the air, which would block the sun's rays from the surface of the planet for years. As plants withered from lack of sunlight, ecosystems would collapse and extinction would be widespread, especially among larger animals like dinosaurs and pterosaurs. Several lines of evidence support this theory, including a concentration of the element Iridium in rocks at the top of the Upper Cretaceous sequence. Iridium is rare on Earth, but often found in high concentrations in meteorites and asteroids.

Attempts to Make Pterosaurs Fly Again

Pterosaur models have helped us better understand how pterosaurs flew. But building models can never be a perfect practice because we cannot mechanically reproduce the subtle movements possible for living tissue, and we cannot control a model's responses to the same degree a pterosaur's brain could. Still, inflexible pterosaur models tested in wind tunnels have given us some insight into why pterosaurs were so successful.

In 1956, a *Rhamphorhynchus* model was constructed from rice paper, balsa wood, rubber bands and aluminum at the Max Planck Institute for Behavioral Physiology in Germany. The model flapped its wings two to three times per second and then glided languidly to the ground. The flight was apparently quite elegant, more like that of a bird than a bat.

More extensive and expensive experiments were conducted after the discovery of *Quetzalcoatlus*. Under the guidance of Paul MacCready, an aeronautical engineer, a team of more than a dozen engineers and scientists built a working model of this gigantic pterosaur in 1985 at a cost of more than half a million dollars. With no tail to counterbalance its huge head and long neck, it was necessary to add a tail boom to get the model safely into the air. But once sufficient altitude had been reached, the boom was dropped, and the reconstructed pterosaur flew freely, with head, wing and wing-finger movements radio-controlled from the ground.

Pterosaurs in Fiction and Film

Not just scientists' imaginations have been captivated by the pterosaur. Speculation about pterosaur lives has led to imaginative portrayals of what life would be like if they were still among us.

The reputation of pterosaurs in fiction has not fared well. Although they have not captured as much attention as dinosaurs in imaginative fiction, they nevertheless are well represented in novels, comics and movies. While *Tyrannosaurus rex* reigns supreme as king of the dinosaur monsters in fiction, *Pteranodon* is unquestionably king of the pterosaur villains.

Among major works of fiction, one of the earliest pterosaur appearances was in Sir Arthur Conan Doyle's *The Lost World*, published in 1912. Doyle's Professor Challenger not only finds pterosaurs in a remote corner of South America, but even captures a live specimen to bring back to London. Edgar Rice Burroughs used pterosaurs in several of his prehistoric worlds, but perhaps his most frightening vision was of a society of saurian rulers called Mahars at the center of the earth. These hideous *Rhamphorhynchus*-like creatures were highly intelligent, built cities, kept books and used humans for slaves and ritualistic sacrifices.

Pterosaurs established themselves early in the motion picture industry in such classics as the 1925 film adaptation of *The Lost World* and the 1933 version of *King Kong. Rodan, the Flying Monster* depicted perhaps the most famous movie pterosaur. Created by the Japanese filmmakers who brought the world Godzilla, Varan and Mothra in the 1950s and 60s, Rodan was an unlikely looking supersonic flier with disproportionately stubby wings for its gigantic dimensions.

Pterosaurs made their cartoon debut in 1912 in *Gertie the Dinosaur,* the first animation film ever released. In Walt Disney's 1940 animated classic *Fantasia,* mosasaurs captured pterosaurs soaring over the sea. Though often portrayed as villainous monsters, pterosaurs have had more functional and humorous roles in the Hanna-Barbara television series *The Flintstones,* in which they served as airliners. Pterosaurs also have figured heavily in comic book tales involving dinosaurs and other prehistoric animals, with classic images appearing in series like *Tarzan of the Apes; Kona, Monarch of Monster Isle;* and *Turok, Son of Stone.* Imaginative filmmakers and comic book illustrators have even looked to the future and created a robot pterosaur for *Dinobots.*

The
Rhamphorhynchoid Pterosaurs

THE FIRST VERTEBRATE FLIERS

SCAPHOGNATHUS

*R*hamphorhynchoid pterosaurs were the first vertebrates capable of powered flight. They appeared 225 million years ago during the Late Triassic Period in southern Europe. This was an important time in the earth's history because flying reptiles, dinosaurs and mammals appeared almost simultaneously. At that time, a number of previously successful animals, including the mammal-like reptiles and thecodonts, the common ancestor of dinosaurs and pterosaurs, were facing extinction. Rhamphorhynchoids reached peak diversity 75 million years later. The more advanced aerialists, the pterodactyloids, had appeared by then and shortly after out-competed the rhamphorhynchoids and put them on the path toward extinction.

A rhamphorhynchoid's skull is huge, almost equaling the length of its body. The face is short, and the nostrils are usually small and close to the midpoint of the skull. The eye sockets, positioned directly over the joint of the jaw, are huge, and indicate that rhamphorhychoids may have had stereoscopic vision. Between the eye and the external nostril is an extra opening, called an antorbital fenestra, to help keep the skull's weight to a minimum. Ten to twenty enamel-covered teeth line each jaw.

Rhamphorhynchoids have relatively short necks, but their long tails can have up to 40 vertebrae. The tail was stiffened by long tendons, which probably kept it from dragging in the water as the pterosaur skimmed just above the surface. The wrist bones are short, and the finger bones tend to be longer than the bones of the toes.

Rhamphorhynchoids are best known from marine fossil beds in Europe, although fragmentary remains have been discovered on almost every continent. Fish formed the diet of most known rhamphorhynchoids. Their remains are frequently associated with fish fossils, and their intermeshing teeth were ideal for trapping slippery prey.

A typical rhamphorhynchoid is *Rhamphorhynchus*. Because of the remarkable preservation of detail in the lithographic limestones of Solnhofen, Germany, we know much about its soft anatomy. The wing membrane, preserved in more than a dozen specimens, did not extend to the feet as it does in bats. As Harry Govier Seeley pointed out almost a century ago, most pterosaur drawings incorrectly show the wing membrane attached to the ankle. The membrane extended only from the wingtip to the hips, leaving the hind legs free for walking or running. The membrane is not smooth, but has ridges supported by a system of fibers, which may have been cartilaginous rods. The fibers are oriented backward and outward from the supporting wing finger in a pattern similar to a bird's flight feathers. This similarity is strictly functional, however, and allowed both types of animals to fold their wings against their bodies.

The wing membrane of Rhamphorhynchus was strengthened by fibers arranged like the spokes of a folding fan.

Scientists once thought that the leathery wings of pterosaurs, like *Rhamphorhynchus*, were poorly adapted because they seemed highly susceptible to injury. Once the skin was torn, it was assumed the animal would not be able to fly anymore. However, supporting struts would not only have made the wing tougher, but would also have allowed the pterosaur to fly even with minor injuries.

A vertical flap of skin at the end of the tail of Rhamphorhynchus was supported by cartilaginous extensions from the vertebrae.

The tail of *Rhamphorhynchus*, longer than the head and body combined, has a vertical flap of skin, sometimes diamond-shaped, at its tip. Although its function is not known, it may have steered the animal in flight or propelled it through the water.

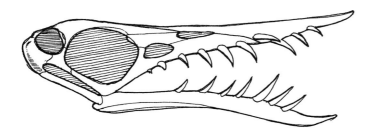

The fearsome-looking skull of Rhamphorhynchus *(top)* has forward-curving teeth that intermesh when the jaws are closed *(middle)*. The sharply pointed tips of the jaws contain no teeth and were probably covered by birdlike beaks *(bottom)*.

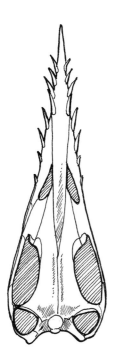

PREONDACTYLUS BUFFARINII

In 1982, Nando Buffarini discovered an almost complete pterosaur skeleton in the 220-million-year-old limestones of Italy's Preone Valley. *Preondactylus* was a medium-sized rhamphorhynchoid with a wingspan of one and a half meters. The discovery was exciting and of great scientific importance. With the longest hind limbs but shortest wings known for a pterosaur, *Preondactylus* may be the most primitive pterosaur yet discovered. The long hind limbs indicate it was well-adapted for walking, and its discovery lends support to the theory that pterosaurs evolved flight from the ground up. As in other pterosaurs, the wing finger has four joints. The bone nearest the tip of the wing may hold a clue to the origin of pterosaur flight. Because it is longer than the others, it has been suggested that the evolution of the wing-supporting structure began here. Then elongation worked back through the other joints of the wing, and eventually the bones of the wrist and lower arm became longer in more advanced species.

A BEACH IS THE SCENE OF THE elaborate mating dance between a pair of *Preondactylus*. Whether this primitive pterosaur behaved this way is uncertain, but such displays are ancient and widespread in the animal kingdom because they ensure the suitability of a potential mate.

EUDIMORPHODON RANZII

Specimens of *Eudimorphodon* have been found in 220-million-year-old marine rocks near Bergamo, Italy. *Eudimorphodon* was a somewhat primitive rhamphorhynchoid pterosaur, but its longer wings and shorter legs place it an evolutionary step ahead of *Preondactylus*. Its tail was as long as its body and may have been used to propel itself in the water and steer itself in the air. Unlike other pterosaurs, the teeth of *Eudimorphodon* are not simple cones. As many as five cusps appear on each adult tooth. Juveniles have fewer teeth in a shorter snout, and the maximum number of cusps is three. Multi-cusped teeth are unusual in reptiles and may indicate that *Eudimorphodon* chopped its prey into small pieces before swallowing.

Fossilized stomach contents prove *Eudimorphodon* ate fish, mostly *Parapholidophorus*, which is believed to have lived in warm Triassic lagoons. Although *Eudimorphodon* probably hunted from the air, its feet suggest it was a capable swimmer, and it may have been able to pursue prey on or under the water.

THE WARM LAGOONS OF TRIASSIC Italy were the hunting ground of *Eudimorphodon*. Diving into the water at high speed, it attempts to catch a fish its sharp eyes have spotted from the air. *Eudimorphodon* was relatively small, with a wingspan of about one meter.

DIMORPHODON MACRONYX

In 1829, William Buckland, the man who found the first dinosaurs, collected the first specimen of *Dimorphodon* from 210-million-year-old rocks at Lyme Regis, England. The name *Dimorphodon*, established almost four decades later by Sir Richard Owen, means "two types of teeth" and refers to the front teeth of the upper jaws being longer than the back ones. Most teeth in the lower jaws are small and close set. The front teeth were probably used to grab prey, while the back ones sliced it up. The species name, *D. macronyx,* means "large puncture" and refers to its large sharply recurved claws.

Like other rhamphorhynchoids, *Dimorphodon* was mostly head and tail. The skull is 20 centimeters long and lightly constructed, with large openings, including those for nostrils and eyes. The tail is as long as the combined length of the head and the rest of the body. The flat of the foot, between the ankle and toes, is short, but the length of the leg indicates *Dimorphodon* was an agile runner. Harry Govier Seely first proposed this idea, and Kevin Padian has subsequently studied it intensively.

Dimorphodon remains are associated with the fossils of land animals such as the armored dinosaur *Scelidosaurus.* It is possible *Dimorphodon,* unlike most known pterosaurs, hunted land-dwelling animals.

ATTACKING A LIZARD FROM TWO fronts, a *Dimorphodon* pair is equally at home on the ground or in the air. Their daggerlike front teeth will make short work of the hapless lizard. The Early Jurassic fossil record of lizards is poor, but they were evidently going through rapid evolutionary diversification.

DORYGNATHUS BANTHENSIS

The first *Dorygnathus* specimen, described in 1830, was recovered from the 190-million-year-old rocks near Banz, Germany. These rocks were once sediments in a rich marine environment that was the hunting ground of *Dorygnathus*, a somewhat small rhamphorhynchoid pterosaur with a wingspan of little more than a meter. Although not as common as *Rhamphorhynchus*, it was similar in most respects. The name *Dorygnathus*, meaning "spear jaw," suited it well. When this pterosaur hunted fish, the short spearlike tip projecting from the front of its lower jaws cleaved the surface of the water like the hands of a diver as the head struck downward. Long, deadly and forward-sloping teeth in the upper and lower jaws then impaled the prey, after which *Dorygnathus* pulled its head from the water and continued its flight.

SKIMMING THE SURFACE of the water, *Dorygnathus* surprises a pholidophorid, a primitive type of teleost fish. Most of the thousands of species of modern fish are of the teleost type.

RHAMPHORHYNCHUS LONGICAUDATUS

Rhamphorhynchus is one well-known pterosaur from the Late Jurassic of Europe and Africa. The name *Rhamphorhynchus longicaudatus* means "crooked beak-nose with a long tail," referring to the shape of its pointed upturned snout and long tail. More than six species have been described, all relatively small, with a wingspan of less than a meter. Most specimens have been recovered from the same rocks that produced the first bird, *Archaeopteryx*, indicating that birds and pterosaurs coexisted for at least 90 million years. These rocks were formed at the bottom of an ancient seaway covering much of central Europe, so *Rhamphorhynchus* undoubtedly spent much time skimming the water while searching for fish. Fish are slippery game for the aerial hunter, and *Rhamphorhynchus* had to evolve jaws equal to the challenge. The long sharply pointed teeth of both its upper and lower jaws sloped forward to create a deadly trap for fish. Several fossil specimens have been found with fish scales and bones in the stomach region.

AT THE END OF A SUCCESSFUL HUNT, *Rhamphorhynchus* pulls out of a dive and prepares to fly back to its roost. This flying reptile was a wide-ranging and successful genus well suited to life in a variety of Late Jurassic environments. Most species are known from the marine limestones of Solnhofen in Germany, but one type has been described from the dinosaur-bearing rocks of Tanzania in Africa.

SORDES PILOSUS

A small pigeon-sized pterosaur from the Karatau Mountains of Kazakhstan was described by Russian palaeontologist A. G. Sharov in 1971. Although this region is in central Asia now, 140 million years ago it was near the southwest coast of the continent. *Sordes* is particularly interesting because dense and thick hairlike material, up to half a centimeter long, covered much of its body. Its hairy covering extended from the head to the base of the tail, but covered only the base of each wing. The wing membranes were free and leathery.

The presence of hair in *Sordes* is the first confirmation of a long-held suspicion that pterosaurs were warm-blooded. *Sordes* had an active predatory lifestyle and hair would have insulated the body and reduced drag during flight. It is not known if the hair had the same structure as that of mammals, although this seems unlikely because hair evolved convergently in the two groups. The hair of *Sordes*, like the feathers of birds, may have originally evolved from scales. In pterosaurs, birds and bats, insulation helps to maintain the high constant body temperature necessary for these animals to be active on cooler days or in cooler environments.

Sordes, like other pterosaurs, had a small membrane extending between the wrist and neck. Unlike *Rhamphorhynchus*, the wing membranes attached to the legs, which may have been used to control the tension of the wings during flight. Another membrane stretched between the legs like the uropatagium of modern bats. This membrane was not attached to the tail, which was free to act as a rudder or counterbalance. A long tail gave a pterosaur like *Sordes* more stability in slow flight by counterbalancing the body, thus increasing the angle of the wings and creating more lift.

SIZING UP A POTENTIAL VICTIM, A hairy pterosaur swoops behind an unsuspecting tree frog. Frogs were already very modern in appearance 200 million years ago. Although the earliest known tree frogs were from the Palaeocene, they probably appeared during the Jurassic or Cretaceous.

ANUROGNATHUS AMMONI

The first *Anurognathus* specimen, found in 1922, was recovered from the rich storehouse of Jurassic limestones at Solnhofen, Germany. *Anurognathus* was a tiny pterosaur with a wingspan of only 30 centimeters. Its three-centimeter-long skull is deep and narrow, and has a short face with peglike teeth. Both features suggest hunting techniques different from the long-nosed spear fishers like *Rhamphorhynchus*. *Anurognathus* may have snatched fish from the water with its long hind limbs. The wings of *Anurognathus* were also long for a pterosaur of its size, and the tail was short. The combination of size and body proportions suggests *Anurognathus* was a swift and highly maneuverable flier.

SWOOPING LOW, *Anurognathus* snatches a fish and flaps vigorously to drag it from the water. *Anurognathus* had longer hind limbs than most pterosaurs, which it possibly used for fishing as some birds and bats do today.

The
Pterodactyloid Pterosaurs
THE SECOND WAVE OF FLIERS

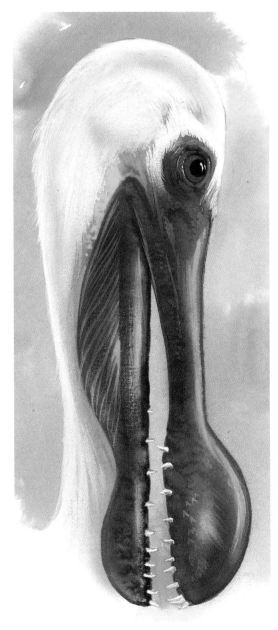

TROPEOGNATHUS

Pterodactyloid pterosaurs, better known as pterodactyls, appeared 50 million years after their ancestors, the rhamphorhychoids, and competed in the Late Jurassic skies for the same marine food sources. The more advanced pterodactyls were the eventual winners in this struggle for aerial supremacy. Rhamphorhynchoids became extinct 145 million years ago, while pterodactyls died out 80 million years later.

Pterodactyls differed from their ancestors in many subtle ways. Pterodactyls had a somewhat longer face, and the nasal opening had moved back to join the opening in front of the eye. The brain was somewhat larger, so the portion of the skull encasing it became inflated. Depending on diet and hunting techniques, pterodactyls' teeth were either more numerous or lost completely.

The pterodactyl's neck was longer and more curved than a rhamphorhynchoid's. The tail was much shorter, giving it greater maneuverability and speed than its predecessor. A larger brain is almost certainly related to this reduction in the length of the tail. A larger brain would be able to compensate for the more rapid changes in flight patterns resulting from a less aerodynamically stable form. The pterodactyl's combination of a large brain and short tail probably gave it the evolutionary advantage over rhamphorhynchoids.

In the most advanced and largest pterodactyls, the wings needed strong braces. The shoulder blade, held in position at the top by muscles in most animals, attached directly to the pterodactyl's backbone, which was fused for strength in this region. The fused vertebrae formed a brace that could withstand the tremendous stresses created by vigorous flapping of their wings.

Most pterodactyls were larger than rhamphorhynchoids, and some had wingspans equal to a twin-engine aircraft. The wing structure of pterodactyloids also gave them an evolutionary advantage over rhamphorhynchoids. The small bones in the wrist of a pterodactyloid fuse into two rows, indicating that movement here was more controlled and that the wing was more stable. The first bone of the wing finger is much longer than the same bone in rhamphorhynchoids. In these more primitive pterosaurs, the last joint of the finger is the longest, but throughout pterosaur evolution, bones progressively closer to the body became longer.

CTENOCHASMA GRACILE

Like so many other pterosaurs described in this book, *Ctenochasma* is from the Upper Jurassic rocks of Germany. Like modern shorebirds, *Ctenochasma* probably fished in waters rich with marine life. Its long jaws, armed with more than 350 small teeth, suggested an obvious name, "comb mouth," when the animal was first described in 1852. The jaws were suitable for catching small fish, but it is also possible *Ctenochasma* used its teeth, like *Pterodaustro,* to strain small invertebrates from seawater.

YOUNG *CTENOCHASMA* eagerly await a meal of fish caught by one of their caring parents. Pterosaurs like *Ctenochasma* were probably social creatures that congregated in flocks.

GNATHOSAURUS SUBULATUS

Gnathosaurus, another example of the rich pterosaur fauna from the Upper Jurassic rocks of Solnhofen, Germany, had an interesting spoon-shaped bill probably used for catching fish. The bill was similar to a spoonbill's, a modern bird that catches frogs, fish and other small swimming animals with its long jaws. While nothing but the skull of *Gnathosaurus* has been recovered, its close relationship to *Ctenochasma* gives us a good idea of what its body looked like. Assuming similar body proportions, a skull 28 centimeters long would result in a wingspan of approximately 1.7 meters.

The top of the skull of *Gnathosaurus* has a long, low and longitudinal crest. A closely related form, *Huanhepterus* from the Ordos basin of China, has a similar crest extending to the front of its skull. The purpose of the head crest is unknown, but it may have helped the animal steer during flight. By turning its head slightly, *Gnathosaurus* would have been able to redirect the flow of air past its body.

LIFE AMONG THE PTEROSAURS MAY have been a colorful affair. We do not know what colors pterosaurs were, but these highly visual animals may have been as brightly colored as many modern birds. The similarity of the bill of *Gnathosaurus* to a spoonbill's inspired this reconstruction.

PTERODAUSTRO GUINAZUI

One of the most highly specialized pterosaurs, *Pterodaustro* was found in 140-million-year-old rocks in Argentina. It was a medium-sized form with a wingspan of less than two meters. Its skull is about 23 centimeters long, but most of this length is made up of its long curved mouth. The lower jaws contain hundreds of long slender teeth, while those of the upper jaw are shorter and broader. The structure of the teeth, reminiscent of the baleen of a whale, may have served a similar function in trapping krill and plankton. Although it seems incredible that a pterosaur the size of an eagle would have become so highly adapted to feeding on such tiny plants and animals, this rich food source also nourishes the largest creature on Earth, the Blue Whale. The curved jaws of *Pterodaustro* allowed it to glide over the water with the tip just skimming the surface. Water pouring into its sievelike mouth was forced to the back of the jaws where krill and plankton were trapped. The upper jaw then closed to force the water out between the teeth before the meal was swallowed.

SKIMMING THE SURFACE OF THE sea, the sievelike lower jaw of *Pterodaustro* drops to scoop up water rich with tiny invertebrates living just beneath the surface. Its jaws and teeth were particularly well adapted to removing this rich source of food from the water.

DSUNGARIPTERUS WEII

Dsungaripterus is an unusual pterodactyloid pterosaur with upturned jaws, the toothless portion of which was probably covered with a horny beak. The beak would have been narrow and pointed, but broad blunt teeth at the back of the jaws may have been suitable for crushing mollusks like clams. Not surprisingly, its bones are usually found in the sediments of ancient lakes. Like many other pterodactyls, it had a distinctive crest on top of its head.

The first good *Dsungaripterus* specimens were discovered in the 1960s in the Junggar Basin of northwestern China where pterosaur fossils are very common. Because *Dsungaripterus* is always found with the dinosaur *Psittacosaurus*, Chinese researchers refer to Lower Cretaceous rocks as the psittacosaur-pterosaur beds. *Dsungaripterus* and a close relative, *Phobetor parvus*, have been found in neighboring regions of Kazakhstan in central Asia and in Mongolia and Romania. A related form also has been identified in South America. Most specimens are small, but wingspans of up to three meters have been reported.

A SMALL DINOSAUR, *PSITTACOSAURUS,* has inadvertently wandered into the periphery of a *Dsungaripterus* colony and is in danger of being attacked by the guards. High concentrations of pterosaur bones provide the best evidence that at least some species gathered in colonies, possibly to protect their young better.

PTERANODON INGENS

One of the largest pterosaurs, *Pteranodon* commonly attained a wingspan of more than six meters. One species, *Pteranodon sternbergi*, may have had a wingspan of more than 10 meters, more than double the size of the largest living bird, the Andean condor. All species of *Pteranodon* had toothless jaws and the pterosaurs' characteristic crest. The crest was variable in shape, and its function is unknown. In some species, it doubled the length of the head and obviously would have had affected the animal's aerodynamics. It may have served, for example, as a brake when *Pteranodon* was landing or as a rudder when it was in flight. It also may have cleaved the water's surface like the prow of a boat when *Pteranodon* captured a fish and had to pull it from the water. Or the crest may simply have counterbalanced the long beak. *Pteranodon* skulls discovered without the characteristic crest may have been from females. If so, yet another function for the crest becomes possible. Males may have used it as a sexual display to attract a mate or to identify other individuals.

Pteranodon skeletons are found in sediments that were hundreds of kilometers from land when the animals were alive. While these huge animals no doubt flapped their wings to gain altitude initially, they probably spent most of their time soaring with their wings motionless. Soaring would have allowed them to travel great distances without expending much energy. By fishing far out to sea, *Pteranodon* would not have had to compete with other pterosaurs that hunted closer to shore. Fish bones make up the fossilized stomach contents of some specimens, so there is no question about the food preferences of *Pteranodon*.

Many specimens of *Pteranodon* were recovered from the Cretaceous chalks of Kansas before the end of the nineteenth century, and new specimens are still being discovered. Although usually crushed because of the softness of the chalk they are buried in, many almost complete skeletons have been recovered, and many species have been described. Species closely related to *Pteranodon* have been found in European rocks of the same age.

HUNDREDS OF KILOMETERS from shore, giant *Pteranodon* circle, waiting for an opportunity to feed on a school of fish driven to the surface by a mosasaur, a huge marine lizard related to the modern Komodo Dragon.

TROPEOGNATHUS MESEMBRINUS

A marvelous variety of well-preserved pterosaurs have been recovered from northeastern Brazil. About 115 million years ago, this region was near the sea. At times it was covered by freshwater lakes, but at other times the sea crept far enough inland to create lagoons teeming with marine life. *Tropeognathus* was one of the fish-eating pterosaur species to inhabit the region. Similarities between the Brazilian and English pterosaurs of the Early Cretaceous suggest *Tropeognathus* enjoyed wide distribution. Detailed comparisons, however, are difficult because the English specimens described more than a century ago are not complete.

The skull of *Tropeognathus* is about 65 centimeters long, with a pair of keels at the front of the jaws, one above the mouth and one below. These were probably covered by horny bills when *Tropeognathus* was alive. Probably a fish-eater, *Tropeognathus* skimmed the surface of the water at high speed, while its jaws lunged into the water to close on prey. The keels helped reduce resistance to the water and increase the stability of the head as *Tropeognathus* pulled fish from the water.

Like some German pterosaur fossils, some specimens from Brazil preserve the body outline, and one even shows evidence of skin or muscle fibers. But Brazilian discoveries show wing membranes attached to the knees rather than the hips as in the German species. This suggests that the more advanced pterosaurs may have been less mobile on land than their earlier close relatives, the rhamphorhynchoids.

SWEEPING ABOVE THE POUNDING SURF, *Tropeognathus* snap up fish brought to the surface by the turbulent waters. This sophisticated pterosaur was probably well adapted for flying at high speeds over the water's surface and catching a meal without losing its momentum. The shape of the lower jaws suggests it had a pouch between the jaws and throat, much like a modern pelican's, to store captured fish.

QUETZALCOATLUS NORTHROPI

Quetzalcoatlus takes its name from the Aztec's feathered serpent-god and its species name, *Q. northropi*, from Northrop's flying wing aircraft. Both names evoke the enormity of this pterosaur, the largest flying animal to have ever lived. The largest specimen has an estimated wingspan of 12 meters, but the scattered remains of more than a dozen specimens half that size have also been recovered. *Quetzalcoatlus northropi* was also one of the last pterosaurs to live before the species became extinct at the end of the Cretaceous.

Besides its great size, *Quetzalcoatlus* is easily identified by its long toothless skull and long neck. Like *Pteranodon*, *Quetzalcoatlus* soared aloft on updrafts and thermals. Its long legs seem relatively weak, but may have been all it needed to leap high enough to catch a passing breeze. Despite its enormous size, a full-grown *Quetzalcoatlus* weighed only as much as an average man!

It is difficult to imagine what kind of food sustained this huge pterosaur. *Quetzalcoatlus* did not live near the sea, so it was probably not a fish-eater. Wann Langston Jr. suggested it foraged on the ground or along the margins of marshes and lakes, using its long slender beak to pick up invertebrates. Others believe the long neck could have evolved for feeding on carrion, allowing it to probe deep into rotting dinosaur carcasses. However, no pterosaur had jaws powerful enough to tear flesh the way a vulture does today.

Quetzalcoatlus may have nested in or near coniferous forests of Cretaceous North America. Masses of coniferous needles and fossilized eggshell fragments have been discovered with several *Quetzalcoatlus* skeletons. In 1972, Douglas Lawson first found the remains of this giant pterodactyloid in the 65-million-year-old rocks of Big Bend National Park in Texas. A closely related form, *Titanopteryx*, was found in the 1940s in Jordan from somewhat older rocks. Other specimens related to *Quetzalcoatlus* have been recovered from Alberta, Montana and Wyoming in North America, and from Uzbekestan in central Asia.

THE GIANT AMONG ANCIENT aerialists, *Quetzalcoatlus* claims the carcass of a horned dinosaur in prehistoric Texas. Dromaeosaurs skulk in the foreground, patiently awaiting an opportunity to seize their share of the carrion.

The
Dinosaurs
AN EVOLUTIONARY PATH TO THE AIR

OVIRAPTOR

*D*inosaurs were the dominant land animals between 225 and 65 million years ago, during which time many species evolved and became extinct. To the average eye, dinosaurs have little in common with birds. But to the trained eye of a scientist, a giant predator like *Tyrannosaurus rex* and the smallest songbird have a common heritage. Tracing the evolutionary adaptations of lizard-hipped theropod dinosaurs provides clues to the mystery of how dinosaurs conquered the air.

Palaeontologists identify the Dinosauria as a group of animals sharing a common ancestor and the following characteristics: 1) the vomer, a bone in the roof of the mouth, is longer than in crocodiles, pterosaurs and other more primitive forms; 2) three or more vertebrae fuse between the hips to form the sacral portion of the backbone; 3) the joint between the shoulder girdle and the arm faces backward; 4) a crest on the upper arm bone for muscle attachment extends at least a third of the length of the bone; 5) the index finger has three or fewer joints; 6) the socket in the hip for the upper leg bone has a large opening on the inside wall; 7) the ball-like head of the upper leg bone is on the inside of the bone and not on top; 8) one of the two bones in the lower leg is much thinner than the other; and 9) one ankle bone, firmly attached to the larger lower leg bone, has a long splint in front of the shin that strengthens the contact. Most of these characters evolved because dinosaurs walked upright with their legs directly beneath their bodies, unlike those reptiles that sprawl. Of course, many other characteristics help identify dinosaurs as a group, but these unique features distinguish them from their closest relatives, including the pterosaurs. Birds, a subset of the Dinosauria, possess all these characters.

Dinosaurs can be divided into two distinct lineages, the bird-hipped ornithischians and the lizard-hipped saurischians. The bird-hipped, plant-eating dinosaurs include ornithopods and dome-headed, horned and armored forms. The ornithopods were mainly large bipedal animals like the duck-billed dinosaurs. Dome-headed dinosaurs, also known as pachycephalosaurids, were smaller bipeds, whose large skulls lent them an intelligent appearance. However, a pachycephalosaurid's brain was small, and the high dome on top of the skull was mostly bone. The horned dinosaurs, or ceratopsians, were rhinoceroslike animals with a crest

The hips of vertebrates –
including theropods, bird-
hipped dinosaurs and birds –
are made up of three pairs of
bones called the ilium, pubis
and ischium. In the most
primitive reptiles, the pubis
points down and forward. Most
theropods have this
arrangement. At the other
extreme, the pubis of birds
(top) has turned backward to
lie beside the ischium. The
pubis of bird-hipped
ornithischian dinosaurs (middle)
also lies beside the ischium, but
a branch of it faces forward.
Lizard-hipped saurischian
dinosaurs like Velociraptor
(bottom) have a very birdlike
pelvis.

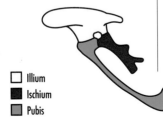

☐ Illium
■ Ischium
■ Pubis

at the back of the skull extending over the neck, a horn over the nose and a pair of horns above the eyes. There were two types of armored dinosaurs. The stegosaurs had vertical spikes and plates of bone standing above the backbone, while ankylosaurs tended to be broader animals with bony plates covering the top of the body and spikes extending from the sides of the body. Some ankylosaurs had bony clubs at the end of their tails. As their name suggests, bird-hipped dinosaurs had a hip structure similar to birds. Once, this similarity was thought to indicate an evolutionary relationship between ornithischian dinosaurs and birds, but it is now clear this is another example of convergent evolution.

The lizard-hipped saurischians were closer to pterosaurs, their first cousins, and to birds, their offspring. Saurischians include two major lineages, the Sauropodomorpha and the Theropoda. Long-necked, long-tailed giants like *Apatosaurus*, *Brachiosaurus* and *Diplodocus* are examples of sauropodomorphs. All meat-eating dinosaurs, large and small, were theropods. Although most theropods had lizardlike hips, some, like *Velociraptor*, had hips indistinguishable from those of primitive birds like *Archaeopteryx*.

Theropods all had the same basic body form, which must have been well suited to a predatory lifestyle because it persisted for 140 million years. They were bipedal like modern birds and humans. Their arms were always shorter than their hind legs, and in some of the most derived forms, such as *Carnotaurus* and *Tyrannosaurus*, the arms were so short as to appear useless. But appearances can be deceiving. Tyrannosaurid arms were longer than human arms and could lift more than 300 kilograms, or the equivalent of three large men. Their deadly claws were long and powerful. Small arms probably evolved as a way to reduce weight at the front of the body. Theropods were like living teeter-totters, with the tail balancing the front of the body. As they got larger, the skull, with its huge teeth, became disproportionately heavy and made it necessary to lose weight in front of the hips.

Although theropods generally look similar, they are as diverse as the seven modern carnivore families, which include dogs, bears, raccoons, weasels, viverrids, hyaenas and cats. There were tiny theropods like *Compsognathus*, giants like *Tyrannosaurus*, crested forms like *Dilophosaurus*, toothless egg-eaters like *Oviraptor*, toothless runners like *Ornithomimus* and large-brained birdlike examples like *Troodon*.

Birds evolved from theropods before the end of the Jurassic, 150 million years ago, but many of the most birdlike theropod specimens date from the Late Cretaceous, 50 to 85 million years later. Although these highly birdlike carnivorous dinosaurs appear too late on the evolutionary clock to have been the ancestors of birds, scientists attribute this to gaps in the earlier fossil record where, as we will see, specimens are frustratingly rare. The Late Cretaceous birdlike dinosaurs nevertheless tell us much about the evolutionary transition from dinosaurs to birds and emphasize how closely birds and theropods are related.

This highly simplified cladogram shows the relationship of theropod dinosaurs to birds. The more primitive forms are shown on the left, and the more advanced are on the right.

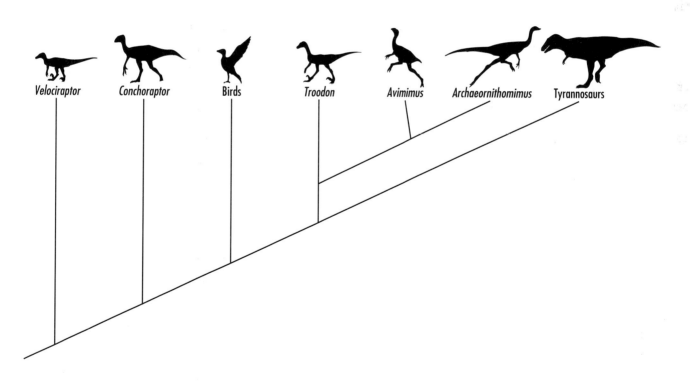

Velociraptor Conchoraptor Birds Troodon Avimimus Archaeornithomimus Tyrannosaurs

COMPSOGNATHUS LONGIPES

Tiny *Compsognathus*, the smallest known theropod, was no bigger than an average chicken. It lived near the shores of lagoons in the warm shallow seas covering much of Late Jurassic Europe. *Compsognathus* was a speedy bipedal predator with an unusually large head for its body. It had only two fingers on each hand, like tyrannosaurids, which convergently evolved this feature 60 million years later.

The first *Compsognathus* specimen was recovered from the Upper Jurassic lithographic limestones of Germany's Solnhofen region, which also produced *Archaeopteryx*. *Compsognathus* was discovered with the fossilized skeleton of a smaller animal in its rib cage. Although it was once thought to be the skeleton of an unborn baby, it is now known to be a small lizard, *Bavarisaurus*, which was obviously the dinosaur's last meal. The ability of *Compsognathus* to catch a darting lizard is a testament to its speed and agility. Besides lizards, *Composgnathus* probably fed on insects and other small animals and may have scavenged dead fish washed up on beaches.

A CONFRONTATION ERUPTS WHEN two rivals, *Archaeopteryx* and *Compsognathus*, simultaneously discover a fish carcass on the beach. Bird and dinosaur are almost evenly matched. Though tiny by dinosaur standards, they were both ferocious predators.

VELOCIRAPTOR MONGOLIENSIS

Velociraptor was a small meat-eating dinosaur living in Asia during the Late Cretaceous. Closely related forms have been discovered in North America in Alberta and Montana. An inhabitant of environments from deserts to coastal regions, *Velociraptor* may have hunted in packs, a highly evolved social behavior. Its large wickedly recurved claw on the inside of each foot was probably used to disembowel its prey. A pair of skeletons found in Mongolia vividly preserve the record of one such confrontation. The meat-eater had attacked and killed a plant-eating *Protoceratops* during a sandstorm. Unfortunately for *Velociraptor*, the dying gesture of *Protoceratops* was to clamp its jaws on the attacker's arm, dooming it to death by suffocation under the shifting sands of a dune.

Originally discovered in 1923, *Velociraptor* remained a poorly known dinosaur until its close relative, *Deinonychus*, was described in 1969. Both were obviously very active predators with large brains. Awareness of this resemblance led John Ostrom of Yale University to wonder if dinosaurs were warm-blooded. Speculation that dinosaurs may have internally controlled their body temperature started earlier, in 1925, and Canadian palaeontologist Loris Shano Russell refined the idea in 1965. Once *Deinonychus* was discovered, however, Robert T. Bakker and others advanced powerful arguments in favor of extending the theory of warm-bloodedness to many other dinosaurs. After years of debate, most palaeontologists now believe small agile theropods were probably warm-blooded, but that most other dinosaurs were not. A few palaeontologists still believe all dinosaurs were cold-blooded, and a few more maintain exactly the opposite. If they were warm-blooded, small predatory dinosaurs such as *Velociraptor* may have evolved insulation to maintain a constant high body temperature, which in turn allowed them to be very active even when the weather was cool. Perhaps feathers initially evolved in dinosaurs as insulation and were secondarily adapted for flight in birds. We may never know the answer.

Velociraptor and its kin are so birdlike that one researcher, Greg Paul, went as far as to suggest they were flightless descendants of a flying animal like *Archaeopteryx*. More recent evidence suggests the contrary. Velociraptorines were somewhat primitive in comparison with other Cretaceous theropods, and their birdlike characteristics are simply another example of convergent evolution.

BOUNDING ACROSS THE SANDS OF THE central Asian desert, a *Velociraptor* pack scans the horizon for potential prey. They will take advantage of their speed, intelligence and nasty sicklelike claws to dispatch a victim quickly. Recent research by Mongolian scientist Antangerel Perle suggests *Velociraptor* hopped with the speed and agility of a kangaroo.

CONCHORAPTOR GRACILIS

Conchoraptor, the latest oviraptorid genus to be recognized, is based on a skull and several partial skeletons from Mongolia. Although *Conchoraptor* was closely related to other carnivorous dinosaurs, it did not have teeth. *Conchoraptor* means "shellfish robber," and Rinchen Barsbold, who originally described this animal, felt the jaws were used to break open clams. But other scientists believe its jaws were too lightly built for this lifestyle.

Oviraptorid skulls in general look deceptively like birds'. When the first oviraptorid dinosaur was discovered in Mongolia in 1923, the skull was fortunately found with the skeleton. Otherwise it would have been identified as a peculiar toothless bird. Such a mistake did happen in 1940 when the lower jaws of a specimen from Dinosaur Provincial Park in Alberta were described as a new bird species. More than 30 years passed before someone recognized that the specimen, *Caenagnathus*, was not a bird, but another type of oviraptorid dinosaur.

The first oviraptorid skeleton was found lying on the eggs of a plant-eating dinosaur, suggesting it was caught and buried by a sandstorm when stealing the eggs. In 1924, Henry Fairfield Osborn named this dinosaur *Oviraptor*, which appropriately means "egg stealer." A second example of *Oviraptor* was discovered on another nest of dinosaur eggs, this one in China. Analysis of new *Caenagnathus* specimens from Alberta is indicating that oviraptorids were best adapted for swallowing eggs and small animals whole, thus eliminating the need for teeth.

STANDING OVER EGGS laid by a plant-eating dinosaur, *Conchoraptor* cautiously surveys the scene for protective parents before slipping off with some eggs into the gathering gloom of a storm.

ARCHAEORNITHOMIMUS ASIATICUS

A 1922 expedition from the American Museum of Natural History collected the remains of *Archaeornithomimus* from a fossil-rich bonebed in the Gobi Desert. The site, near the present-day Chinese city of Erenhot, also yielded the first dinosaurs discovered in central Asia. *Archaeornithomimus* was closely related to other "bird mimic" dinosaurs (ornithomimids) like *Struthiomimus* ("ostrich mimic") and *Dromicieomimus* ("emu mimic"). Like many other theropods, ornithomimids had many birdlike characteristics – including toothless jaws, an inflated braincase and air-filled skull bones that underscore the close relationship between dinosaurs and birds. These medium-sized long-legged dinosaurs were descendants of meat-eating forms that had replaced their teeth with birdlike beaks. In size and general body form, they are similar to ostriches, and all evidence suggests they could run just as fast. Ostriches can reach speeds of 80 kilometers per hour.

THEIR LARGE EYES ALERT TO POTENTIAL PREY in the darkness ahead, a small *Archaeornithomimus* herd races across the moonlit plains of central Asia. The juveniles had longer legs in relation to their bodies so they could match the speed of adults. At least one such herd perished catastrophically, leaving its remains in an extensive bonebed in northern China.

TROODON FORMOSUS

Troodon formosus was an active predator of Late Cretaceous North America, and a similar form, *Saurornithoides*, inhabited central Asia during the same period. Troodontid fossils are extremely rare, but one complete skeleton was collected by a Sino-Canadian expedition in 1989 from Lower Cretaceous rocks in China. Using the complete Chinese skeleton as a guide, palaeontologists are now identifying isolated troodontid bones being recovered from North America and Asia.

Because troodontids were very sophisticated animals, they have attracted much scientific attention. Their large brains were equivalent in size to those of primitive birds and mammals, suggesting a level of intelligence not normally attributed to dinosaurs. The eyes of *Troodon* were directed forward with overlapping fields of view to give them stereoscopic vision, which increases depth perception, a tremendous advantage for finding and capturing prey. The sharply clawed fingers were adapted for precise manipulation, the long hind legs were adapted for speed and the inside toe bore a large raptorial claw similar to that of *Velociraptor*.

Although this speedy highly skilled hunter appeared too late in the fossil record to be an ancestor of birds, it had several remarkably birdlike characteristics in its jaws, teeth, braincase and ears. Even in some of the smallest details of anatomy, it is often very difficult to distinguish such dinosaurs from birds.

USING ITS LIGHTNING-SWIFT reflexes, a troodontid relentlessly closes in on an opossumlike mammal, *Didelphodon coyi*, from the Cretaceous. *Troodon formosus* probably developed its large brain and stereoscopic vision so it could successfully pursue such elusive prey.

TYRANNOSAURUS REX

Tyrannosaurus rex, perhaps the most famous dinosaur, lived in a world where dinosaurs were declining in diversity and number while mammals and birds were increasing. Although some scientists feel that *Tyrannosaurus* was a scavenger, its powerful jaws, teeth and long robust legs suggest *Tyrannosaurus* was born a killer. Very few true scavengers exist in nature, and even jackals and hyaenas are now known to be successful predators. *Tyrannosaurus* would certainly have been an opportunist and dined on the carcasses of other dinosaurs when it found them. But the active life of the hunter was necessary for *Tyrannosaurus*. Scavenging would not have fed its huge body, which could weigh more than six metric tons, or more than the largest recorded African elephant.

It is hard to believe that this gigantic predator, still the largest known land carnivore, could be related to birds. While *Tyrannorsaurus* itself did not give rise to birds, many skeletal features suggest it was a close relative. For example, one peculiarity of the modern bird skull is the presence of air-filled bones associated with the joint between the lower jaws and skull. Among dinosaurs, this character was first noted in a *Tyrannosaurus* skull and is now known in other tyrannosaurids like *Albertosaurus* and *Tarbosaurus*.

SHROUDED BY THE MORNING MISTS OF NORTH America's ancient coastal plain, a towering *Tyrannosaurus* opens its mouth to allow a group of small pterosaurs to pick the meat from between its teeth. Symbiotic behavior, the often unexpected relationship between life forms, is widespread in nature. Today, crocodiles in Africa will open their formidable jaws to allow certain birds to clean their teeth while other birds are considered suitable prey.

The
Birds
THE DINOSAURS OF THE AIR

DIATRYMA

What is a Bird?

*T*oday, we normally have no difficulty separating birds from other groups of animals. After all, birds, even penguins, are the only warm-blooded animals with feathers and wings. Perhaps the most unusual trademark of birds is their highly consistent body form. Living birds are characterized by toothless jaws, a horny beak, an inflated braincase, front limbs transformed into wings or else lost, an upright bipedal stance, a very short bony tail and, of course, feathers.

Identifying birds in the fossil record, however, is difficult for a number of reasons. First, bird feathers rarely fossilize along with the wings, leaving the front limbs of primitive birds looking very much like dinosaur arms. As we have seen, a number of dinosaur fossils were originally identified as birds. Secondly, no reliable undisputed method currently exists for determining whether fossils are from warm-blooded or cold-blooded species. Haversian canals in the bone have often been used to demonstrate warm-bloodedness because they are found today only in birds and mammals. But they may be an indication of growth rates rather than consistently high body temperature. Finally, we cannot eliminate the possibility that some dinosaurs may have evolved feathers simply for insulation.

Despite these difficulties, Jacques Gauthier was able to define the advanced characteristics separating the Avialae, a taxon including *Archaeopteryx* and more advanced birds, from other carnivorous dinosaurs. These characters include an enlarged wishbone (the clavicles), a shoulder blade tapered at the end, very long forelimbs and hands, a tail reduced to 23 or fewer vertebrae and fused foot bones. Only through these very specific details can researchers distinguish between bird and dinosaur anatomies.

Bird feathers may have evolved from scales. Reptilian scales and bird feathers develop in the same region of the skin, suggesting an evolutionary relationship. Modern bird feathers still grade into reptilelike scales on their legs. Scales may have initially become long and leaflike, each supported by a central ridge with side branches (left). The next stage saw the separation of the branches into "leaflets" (middle). Finally, the thin membrane around each branch split on a microscopic scale into the barbs and barbules that help make up a modern bird feather (right).

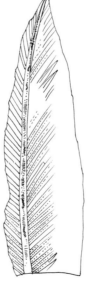

The Origin of Birds

The wishbone found in a chicken or turkey is from the front of the shoulder and chest region. Scientists call it a clavicle. A primitive reptile like Hovasaurus (1) had a large pair of well-developed but unfused clavicles. The fused clavicles of the dinosaur Oviraptor (2), the primitive bird Archaeopteryx (3) and a modern bird (4) show an evolutionary progression supporting the theory that birds evolved from dinosaurs.

1

2

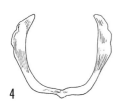

3

4

Nineteenth-century palaeontologists initially accepted that birds evolved directly from meat-eating dinosaurs. But no dinosaurs known during that time were appropriate ancestors because they were already too specialized in many ways. For example, many reptiles, birds and mammals share a primitive character in the presence of a clavicle, better known as the collar bone, in the shoulder girdle. Because highly specialized theropod dinosaurs seem to have lost their clavicles, they could not have been the forerunners of birds unless this bone had reevolved. Once a character has been lost in evolution, it is not likely to evolve a second time. Scientists had to look elsewhere for the beginnings of bird evolution.

Rival theories about bird origins were not long in developing. Early in the twentieth century, it became fashionable to believe that birds and dinosaurs were cousins united by a primitive common ancestor, a group called the thecodonts. The thecodont grade of evolution includes species that looked like meat-eating dinosaurs and forms that gave rise to crocodiles. The theory of birds' thecodont ancestry remained in vogue for more than 50 years.

Zoologists have long known that crocodiles are the closest living relatives of birds. These two groups have similar body traits, many of which are not apparent at first glance. They include the structure of the jaws, ear region, jaw joint and teeth, which many primitive birds had. In 1972, Alex Walker suggested birds may be descendants of the Crocodilia. He was not studying the big sprawling crocodiles and alligators of today, but the smaller species from more than 200 million years ago. Some early crocodilians walked on their hind legs and may even have lived in trees. The theory of a crocodilian origin for birds received much initial support from other scientists.

Around the same time the crocodilian theory of origin was gaining popularity, John Ostrom of Yale University was reexamining the possibility that birds evolved from theropod dinosaurs. By this time, Mongolian palaeontologists had discovered at least some theropods with a clavicle. And many other birdlike characteristics started to emerge in other dinosaurs.

A strong argument in favor of a dinosaurian origin of birds was ironically the incorrect identification of a newly discovered specimen of *Archaeopteryx*, the first undisputed bird. This specimen is almost complete and extremely well preserved, but the feathers had not fossilized. Without feathers, *Archaeopteryx* looked like a dinosaur and was identified as *Compsognathus* for almost a quarter of a century.

All the supposedly unique characters used to show relationship between crocodiles and birds have also been found in dinosaurs, so there is nothing to prove that birds are more closely related to crocodiles than to dinosaurs. Jacques Gauthier listed over 120 unique characteristics found in birds and dinosaurs, but in no other vertebrates, including thecodonts and crocodiles. Although a few scientists are still not convinced, most assert that birds are the direct descendants of carnivorous dinosaurs. In fact, the cladistic analysis of advanced characters, as we have seen, clearly places birds within the Dinosauria.

Other theories proposed for bird origins have never been widely accepted. The idea that pterosaurs gave rise to birds is an obvious one since these two active fliers share many features. But large

One similarity between crocodiles and birds is their teeth. The teeth found in extinct primitive birds like Hesperornis *(1) resemble crocodile teeth (2) in having a constriction between the root and crown. Theropod teeth, like those of* Velociraptor *(3) and* Troodon *(4), have serrations to slice meat. The similarities and differences seem obvious. Recently, however, it was discovered that* Troodon *teeth have a constriction between the root and crown just like primitive bird teeth, and a bird tooth was discovered with serrations just like a dinosaur tooth. This evidence underscores that dinosaurs have a closer evolutionary relationship to birds than do crocodiles.*

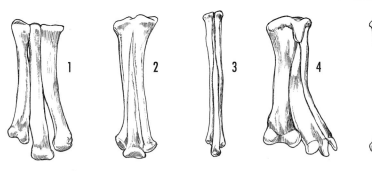

The evolutionary mosaic stretching between dinosaurs and birds is seen in their foot bones. Both birds and dinosaurs have three major toes. The bones of the flat of the foot, the metatarsus, supporting these toes are separate from one another in most theropods (1) and fused in most birds (5). In theropods like Elmisaurus *(2), these bones have fused at the top, while in* Archaeopteryx *(3) they have not. Many foot bones in early birds, such as enantiornithines from the Cretaceous of Argentina (4), are intermediate in their degree of fusion.*

brains, air-filled bones, warm-bloodedness and other characters in birds and pterosaurs can almost always be attributed to convergent evolution in response to similar lifestyles or to inheritance of the same characters from their common ancestor. Generally, flight in pterosaurs and birds is so different that neither could have evolved from the other. Birds' immediate ancestors also have been sought among very ancient reptiles once called eosuchians, which were ancestral to a wide variety of animals, including lizards, snakes, plesiosaurs, crocodiles, dinosaurs and birds. One example, *Cosesaurus*, a small animal from Spain, had large eyes and a birdlike beak but relatively little else to recommend it as a potential protobird.

Bird Flight

Whether bird flight originated from the ground up or from the trees down has been a long-standing argument among scientists. As early as 1879, Samuel Wendel Williston speculated that birds' ability to fly evolved from animals adapted for running on the ground. One year later, Othniel Charles Marsh suggested bird flight originated in tree-dwelling forms.

Bird wings are simply modified arms, and a clear structural transition occurs from dinosaurs to *Archaeopteryx* to modern birds. Until recently, most palaeontologists felt bird flight originated when animals living high in the trees evolved wings for parachuting or gliding. According to this theory, flight evolved as a progression from climbing animals to parachuters to gliders and eventually to active fliers, and wings became progressively larger and more complex with each adaptation. But some scientists have pointed out the flaw in this reasoning: climbing animals' arms function much differently from wings, and it is unlikely wings could evolve from arms specialized for climbing. Also, many animals, from frogs to rodents, have become proficient gliders but have never developed active flapping flight, even after millions of years.

Bones in bird wings (right) evolved from the arms of theropod dinosaurs (left), and the most noticeable adaptation is the fused wrist and hand elements. The feathered wings of Archaeopteryx (middle) were not externally distinguishable from a modern bird's, but the underlying bone structure is virtually identical to a theropod arm.

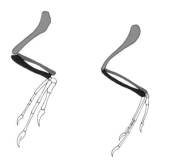

The claw on the third finger of Archaeopteryx has a bone (equivalent to the bone at the end of our finger) and a horny sheath (equivalent to our fingernail). It is long, sharply curved and ends in a needlelike point appropriate for climbing trees.

The rival theory suggests birds evolved from small reptilian species that ran on their hind legs, thus freeing their arms to evolve into wings. The feathers, which are actually highly modified scales, became elongated to help it capture insects or to help the animal run faster as it flailed its arms. It has been proposed that reptilian bird ancestors first used their wings like butterfly nets.

We do not know whether bird flight started on the ground or in the trees. However, the "tree down" theory still has the most widespread support because the evidence is stronger and intuitively this seems a more likely evolutionary path.

John Ostrom suggested feathered wings initially evolved as a net to capture insects. As feathers became longer, the secondary purpose, flight, may have increased in importance.

A
Bird or Dinosaur?
A QUESTION OF IDENTITY

PROTOAVIS

There will never be any doubt about a screeching crow being a bird or a lumbering ankylosaur being a dinosaur. But animals close to the transition from dinosaurs to birds are much more difficult to classify as one or the other. This difficulty is especially apparent, as we have seen, when fossil specimens are incomplete. For example, we are reminded of the confusion surrounding the classification of *Caenagnathus*. Not until a close relationship between it and *Oviraptor*, its close look-alike, was pointed out did scientists realize it was a dinosaur and not a bird.

One such transitional animal may be the one that left small footprints 200 million years ago in what is now Lesotho, in southern Africa. P. Ellenberger described them in 1974 as the footprints of a carnavian (a carnivorous bird) that preceded *Archaeopteryx* by at least 50 million years. But few scientists have seen the original specimens, and most feel the connection between the impressions and the footprints cannot yet be proved.

Serious arguments about the history of bird evolution center on the fossils of *Protoavis* and *Avimimus*, two possible early birds. Both are based on specimens more complete than a few isolated bones or footprints. *Protoavis* has been described as a bird that appeared in the fossil record at least 75 million years before *Archaeopteryx*, but its classification is controversial. *Avimimus* was originally classified as a bird that appeared later than *Archaeopteryx*, but its anatomy was more primitive. Our understanding of the early history of bird evolution changes dramatically if *Protoavis* and *Avimimus* are classed as birds. *Archaeopteryx* specimens, which fortunately include complete skeletons with feather impressions, leave little doubt about the status of *Archaeopteryx* as a bird.

Protoavis was a small birdlike animal. No feather impressions were found with its remains, and its most birdlike characters are also found in theropods. Until more detailed specimens are discovered, its classification as a bird or dinosaur will remain controversial.

PROTOAVIS

In 1986, palaeontologists were intrigued by the discovery of new fossils from the 225-million-year-old rocks of Texas. The discoverer, Sankar Chatterjee of Texas Tech University, had found a bipedal animal not much longer than half a meter from its nose to the tip of its tail. Its small sharp teeth suggest it was an insect-eater. Our knowledge of it comes from two, possibly three, incomplete skeletons, which include a wishbone, a breastbone, clawed fingers and a long tail. Some skull features, such as air-filled bones surrounding the ear and brain, are very birdlike, but these are also found in theropod dinosaurs like *Troodon*.

Sankar Chatterjee claimed that the fossils were the remains of a primitive bird. At a convention that year, hundreds of vertebrate palaeontologists filled a lecture hall, spilling out into the aisles and the halls, to hear him present the evidence. If *Protoavis*, which means "first bird," was a true avian, then birds appeared at least 75 million years earlier than was previously supposed. Not all scientists agree that *Protoavis* was a bird. Many feel it may have been a dinosaur or even a more primitive reptile. If additional research proves the avian status of *Protoavis*, then birds are as ancient as the dinosaurs, with a history stretching back 225 million years.

SCRAMBLING UP THE SIDE OF A tree, a small protobird searches for insects to feed its metabolic furnaces. Feathers probably evolved originally to insulate such an animal, and only later became long enough to allow it to glide and then eventually to fly.

AVIMIMUS PORTENTOSUS

Avimimus was a turkey-sized animal living in central Asia 80 million years ago. Its remains are common at some dinosaur localities in China and Mongolia where they are associated with a range of environments from riverside woodlands to desert margins. A single but distinctive bone found in Dinosaur Provincial Park in Alberta suggests this unusual animal also lived in North America.

Its toothless beak, inflated braincase, wide pelvis, and fused wrist and ankle bones suggest *Avimimus* was a bird. But many of its bones are very similar to a small carnivorous dinosaur's, and some characteristics, such as the structure of the backbone and the vestige of a fifth toe, are too primitive to be found in birds. When *Avimimus* was first discovered at Erenhot in northern China, it was mistakenly identified as the small theropod *Elmisaurus*. Although the mistake was corrected before it became a problem, it does emphasize again the difficulty of distinguishing between the anatomies of birds and dinosaurs.

BIRDLIKE *AVIMIMUS* quickly seeks shelter when the tyrannosaurid *Alectrosaurus* hunts in the area. The remains of both animals were found at Erenhot in northern China by Sino-Canadian expeditions in the late 1980s.

The
Jurassic and Cretaceous Fliers

THE FIRST TRUE BIRDS

ARCHAEOPTERYX

The story of the evolution of birds is filled with many contenders for the status of first bird. We may never know for certain when the earliest bird made its entrance, but we do know that the first modern bird families appeared sometime before the great dinosaur extinction, 65 million years ago. The Late Cretaceous was a time of great evolutionary experimentation in birds, and many models did not survive. This is especially true in South America where enantiornithine birds became very diverse. Once more progressive birds invaded South America, enantiornithines lost the battle for survival and died out.

Disputes have arisen over when modern bird families first made their appearance on the evolutionary stage. The period between the Late Jurassic and Early Cretaceous, 150 to 125 million years ago, was critical to the evolution of birds. The earliest undisputed bird, *Archaeopteryx*, dates from this period. *Archaeopteryx* was essentially a small meat-eating dinosaur with feathers and wings. Over the next 25 million years, flying birds changed dramatically, and some scientists have concluded that many modern birds must have already coexisted with *Archaeopteryx*, making it a relic in its own time. But evidence of more modern birds from the Jurassic and Early Cretaceous is frustratingly sparse, consisting mostly of feathers and footprints. The specimen that will fill the fossil gap and solve this mystery has yet to be found.

Seven *Archaeopteryx* fossils, ranging from complete skeletons to a single feather, provide scientists with a very detailed record of its anatomy. All the specimens were discovered near

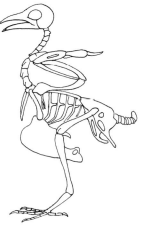

Over long periods, bird skeletons have undergone progressive improvements. Archaeopteryx (left) has teeth in its jaws, a long tail, small breastbone, dinosaurlike fingers and unfused bones in the flat of the foot. The breastbone of an undescribed species from China (middle) has become larger and the tail is shorter. Modern birds, like the pigeon (right), have lost their teeth and evolved an enormous breastbone and fused bones in their hands and feet.

This highly simplified cladogram shows the interrelationships of some major groups of birds. The more primitive birds are on the left, and the more advanced forms are on the right.

Solnhofen, Germany, by workers painstakingly splitting limestone into the thin sheets of stone once used as plates in the lithographic printing process, but now mostly used as shingles. The first *Archaeopteryx* specimen was a partial skeleton discovered in 1855, but scientists mistakenly identified it as a pterosaur. This error was not corrected for 115 years, so most people attribute the first specimen to a single feather impression found in 1860. The following year, the first complete skeleton with clear feather impressions was collected. It was sold two years later to the British Museum of Natural History in London for 700 pounds sterling, a great sum of money at that time. The next specimen, collected in 1877, was a beautiful skeleton with skull and feather impressions that found its way to Humboldt University in Berlin. An equally beautiful fossil was discovered in 1950 and identified for 13 years as *Compsognathus* because it lacked feather impressions. A fragmentary skeleton recovered in 1955 rests in a private collection in Germany and is not available for scientific study. A final skeleton came to palaeontologists' attention in a private collection in 1987 where it also had been mistakenly identified as *Compsognathus*. The specimen, the largest yet discovered, now resides at the Burgermeister-Muller-Museum in Solnhofen, Germany.

Charles Darwin's theories of evolution were given a significant boost by the discovery in 1861 of the first complete *Archaeopteryx* skeleton with feather impressions. Two years before, he had published his book with the unwieldy title *On the Origin of Species by Means of Natural Selection, or the Preservation of Favored Races in the Struggle for Life*. In it, he set out his theory of the mechanism by which evolutionary change occurred. Darwin's studies had convinced him that species were not fixed, but changed through gradual stages into new species. Driving evolutionary change was natural selection, the process by which random variations in the characteristics of species are favored in particular circumstances. A longer sharper claw, for instance, may give an individual a competitive edge in its struggle for survival, and if its offspring inherit this enhancement, they will have a better chance of surviving long enough to produce offspring of their own. Through time, and many such evolutionary advancements, a species gradually changes to the point that it becomes a new species.

Much as Darwin suspected, his theories were greeted with a storm of controversy. His critics were quick to pounce on the weakest point of his case. If new life forms descended from ancient ones, where in the fossil record were the transitional forms that bridged the gap between modern species and their ancestors? Darwin had anticipated this argument and attempted to explain it by inevitable gaps in the fossil record. Fossils, after all, form only in ideal conditions, and Darwin was confident that so-called "missing links" would be discovered.

And suddenly, there was *Archaeopteryx*, clearly neither a modern bird nor an ancient dinosaur, but sharing characteristics of both. Had the feather impressions not been present, this animal would undoubtedly have been described as a dinosaur rather than a bird. The case for the "missing link" could be made.

Dozens of scientific papers have been published on the seven *Archaeopteryx* specimens. Short of some fossils of prehistoric man, no other palaeontological specimens have received so much attention. An animal as famous as *Archaeopteryx* will inevitably become the center of controversy, especially when it is such a keystone to our understanding of bird origins and indeed of evolution itself. Most controversies surrounding *Archaeopteryx* have focused on differences of interpretation of its anatomy. Some scientists questioned whether *Archaeopteryx* was sophisticated enough to fly and wondered if it was restricted to gliding between trees. But analysis of its feathers clearly shows it was a flying animal. Others questioned whether *Archaeopteryx* should be classified as a bird or as a doomed offshoot of the Dinosauria. But the most ludicrous controversy came when a group of physicists led by Sir Fred Hoyle suggested the fossilized feathers of *Archaeopteryx* were a hoax! Although their claim demonstrated their poor understanding of the specimens and of palaeontological techniques, it did create much press until the feathered fossil's authenticity was proved.

ARCHAEOPTERYX LITHOGRAPHICA

About the size and weight of an adult chicken, *Archaeopteryx* was essentially a Late Jurassic dinosaur with feathers. *Archaeopteryx* had teeth in its jaws, a long bony tail and three free fingers with claws. Its toes were relatively blunt, which suggests they were not used for climbing. *Archaeopteryx* feathers are asymmetrical, with the supporting vein closer to the front than the back. Such asymmetrical feathers, found only in flying birds, clearly show *Archaeopteryx* was an active flier and not simply a glider or runner.

All *Archaeopteryx* specimens have been found in sediments deposited 140 million years ago in a lagoon lying between an island landmass and a coral reef, and bordering a shallow sea then covering much of Europe. The specimens may be the remains of unfortunate animals that perished after being blown out to sea by storms. Despite the fossils' location, it is certain *Archaeopteryx* spent much of its time on land, even if the land was little more than a series of islands. Undisputed *Archaeopteryx* specimens have not been found in any other localities, but it is assumed it had a much wider distribution.

Plant remains found in the Solnhofen lithographic limestones indicate the region's climate was tropical, but normally very dry and punctuated at certain times of the year by monsoons sweeping in from the southeast. The main habitat of the early birds was probably a bushland of low conifers.

Archaeopteryx probably fed on insects and other small animals. One scientist proposed it fed on fish and aquatic invertebrates by working its way along the shoreline and using its outstretched wings to shade the water in the same manner as modern herons and egrets.

RETURNING WITH ANOTHER STICK to add to the structure of the nest, an *Archaeopteryx* male waits patiently as his mate prepares to fly off on a similar errand. We do not know if *Archaeopteryx* nested in trees, but nest building is an ancient art practiced even by the dinosaurs.

AN UNNAMED SPECIES FROM CHINA

Some important scientific discoveries are not made by scientists. In 1987, a ten-year-old farm boy discovered a fossil in Liaoning in northeastern China, an area well known for its fossil fish. The shales of the region were once the bottom of a freshwater lake situated 300 kilometers from the sea. But the boy's discovery was no fish. The skeleton, from a small long-limbed animal with a short tail, was clearly a new species of primitive bird. The 140-million-year-old specimen found its way into the collections of the Beijing Natural History Museum and from there journeyed to Chicago where Chinese and American scientists are studying it. Another expedition led by Hou Lianhai from the Institute of Vertebrate Palaeontology and Palaeoanthropology in Beijing in 1990 produced another nine partial skeletons.

The new bird was similar to *Archaeopteryx,* but more advanced in some features. It retained teeth in its jaws, scales across its stomach, claws on its fingers and unfused bones in the flat of its foot. But the breastbone had turned from cartilage to bone and displayed a prominent keel for the attachment of large flight muscles. Like modern birds, the tail was short and many vertebrae were fused into the single bone called a pygostyle, which served as the attachment point for the tail feathers. The structure of the hands and feet and the presence of long, recurved and sharply pointed claws strongly suggest this was a tree-dwelling bird capable of perching.

PERCHING AT THE EDGE OF ITS NEST, a small toothed bird eyes its ravenous young before dropping them a tasty morsel. The forests of northeastern China were not suitable for plant and animal fossilization, but fortunately some carcasses found their way into lakes where they could be buried by sand and mud.

ILERDOPTERYX

This small flying bird inhabited the Early Cretaceous forests of what is now Spain. Lakes in the region captured a sample of the local fauna and flora, preserving them in their limy muds. Plants, insects, salamanders, frogs, turtles and lizards have been recovered from the same rocks as *Ilerdopteryx* and show that the climate was warm and moist.

Ilerdopteryx is intermediate between *Archaeopteryx* and later birds. Unfortunately, no skull has been recovered, and it is not known if *Ilerdopteryx* retained teeth. Its body and tail were shorter than those of *Archaeopteryx*, although it still has more vertebrae than modern birds. The last vertebrae have fused into the pygostyle found in modern birds. The sophisticated shoulder girdle, with its large breastbone, indicates *Ilerdopteryx* was a strong flier. The hind limb, however, is primitive and exhibits little of the bone fusion characteristic of modern birds and even some dinosaurs. Clearly birds' front limbs, or wings, were evolving more rapidly than their legs. Their mobility in the air had become superior to their mobility on the ground.

The small skeleton of *Ilerdopteryx* was claimed in 1985 from 125-million-year-old lake sediments at Las Hoyas ("the Dales") in east-central Spain. Armando Diaz Romeral collected the specimen and subsequently gave it to a museum in Madrid. A formal scientific description of the skeleton has not yet appeared, although a scientific paper was published on *Ilerdopteryx* feathers discovered in rocks of the same age in another region of Spain.

THREATENED BY *PACHYRHACHIS*, AN animal probably intermediate between varanoid lizards and snakes, this Early Cretaceous bird from Spain rises into the air to counterattack. With a tail much shorter than that of *Archaeopteryx*, it may have been a more maneuverable flier.

The Last Toothed Fliers
THE RELICS OF THE CRETACEOUS

Ichthyornis

*B*y the Late Cretaceous, 80 million years ago, modern-looking birds had appeared. Many were charadriiforme types, which include most shorebirds and gulls. More primitive toothed birds, however, were still flying the skies, although their fossil record from this time is depressingly poor. The best representative of toothed birds, *Ichthyornis*, was described more than a hundred years ago from several skeletons found in rocks of marine origin. *Ichthyornis* was probably a fishing bird living near the sea.

A second animal, *Apatornis celer*, is distantly related to *Ichthyornis*. Unfortunately, the fossil is too fragmentary to show if *Apatornis* had teeth. In Alberta, specimens of an eagle-sized flying bird have been recovered recently in Dinosaur Provincial Park. Although this is a distinct species, it does appear closely related to *Apatornis*.

In 1981, Cyril Walker from the British Museum of Natural History described a new subclass of flying birds named the enantiornithines, meaning "opposite birds." They are most easily recognized by their primitive partially fused foot bones, but very specialized bones in the shoulder girdle and arm exist as well. Enantiornithines were not related to any modern bird forms. The fossil record suggests they were most diverse in Argentina where three distinct groups are known, but specimens also have been reported from other parts of South America and from Asia, Australia and North America. Buenos Aires palaeontologist Luis Chiappe suggested that the absence of modern birds and the abundance of enantiornithine birds during the Late Cretaceous in South America may indicate the isolation of the continent at that time.

Ichthyornis, Apatornis, Gobipteryx and enantiornithines appear to be relics of an early radiation having little or nothing to do with modern birds. They may have been evolutionary experiments forced into extinction by their inability to compete with more progressive birds.

ICHTHYORNIS DISPAR

During the Late Cretaceous, ternlike *Ichthyornis* lived along the shores of inland seas covering much of western North America. Its breastbone, shoulder girdle and wing were much more sophisticated than those of *Archaeopteryx*, and except for its teeth, *Ichthyornis* more closely resembled modern birds. It retained, however, enough primitive characters to show it was not related to any living species. *Ichthyornis* fossils have been found far out from Cretaceous shorelines, suggesting that it flew far out to sea to hunt fish. It could probably set down on the surface of the sea just as gulls, ducks and many other modern birds do.

When Benjamin F. Mudge found the first *Ichthyornis* specimen in Kansas in 1872, Othniel Charles Marsh recognized it as an advanced flying bird with teeth. His description became controversial after 1950 when one researcher suggested that a partial bird skeleton had been combined with the toothed jaw of a baby marine reptile. Recent studies of the original specimen and the discovery of new fossils suggest that Marsh's original interpretation was correct. Most scientists now accept *Ichthyornis* as a toothed flier unrelated to modern bird species. Several species of this gull-sized bird ranged from Alabama and Texas in the south to Alberta and Manitoba in the north.

STARTLED BY THE movements of a dinosaur on shore, a flock of *Ichthyornis* takes to the air. This toothed bird was a strong flier, ranging far out to sea in its search for fish.

An Unnamed Species from Argentina

The bones of a chicken-sized bird were unearthed in 1984 on a university campus in northwestern Patagonia in Argentina. The specimen is complete except for the skull. Because it usually takes many years to study a significant specimen, this bird has not yet been named. The same 75-million-year-old rocks have previously yielded the remains of crocodiles, snakes, theropods and an enantiornithine.

This ancient Argentinean species appears to be an early evolutionary attempt by birds to produce a flightless runner. The arms are only half the length of the hind limb, and the forearm is shorter than the upper arm. No wishbone is present, and the breastbone lacks the characteristic keel of flying birds that anchors the strong flight muscles. This archaic flightless lineage of birds does not have living relatives. Superficially, it seems to have changed little from its theropod ancestors, although it was in reality a descendant of flying bird species.

SCRAMBLING THROUGH THE SHALLOW water, a small flightless bird snaps at a frog in a Patagonia very different from today. No evidence of frogs has been recovered from the same site where this bird was found, but we know these amphibians were extensively distributed during the Cretaceous and may have made appetizing meals.

GOBIPTERYX MINUTA

Gobipteryx was a partridge-sized bird inhabiting the deserts of central Asia. The design of its toothless beak and the arrangement of bones in the roof of its mouth are similar to the beaks and mouths of ostriches and their kin. The skull of *Gobipteryx* is less flexible than a modern bird's, and its unusual lower jaws are fused to each other at the front. In these characters, *Gobipteryx* is less sophisticated than most modern birds, although the forelimb and shoulder girdle suggest it was a competent flier.

Gobipteryx remains were first discovered in 1971 at two major dinosaur-producing localities in Mongolia. Two embryos have been discovered in eggs. The embryos are approximately 40 millimeters long, with the skull making up half their length. Their wings are so well developed that the babies may have been capable of flying within days of hatching. With small predators like *Velociraptor* and *Oviraptor* hunting in the area, safety would have been theirs only in the air.

The discovery of *Gobipteryx* embryos was very fortunate. Thousands of unbroken eggs have been found in central Asia, but almost none contain bones. Apparently, the fluid contents typically digested the embryos before the eggs were fossilized. Other small eggs found in 80-million-year-old rocks in the Gobi Desert have been attributed to *Gobipteryx*. Eggs of this type were found in northern China in small clusters, suggesting *Gobipteryx* laid few eggs. A normal infant mortality rate would have quickly decimated a species that produced such a small number of eggs, so the parents of *Gobipteryx* must have been very protective.

Although *Gobipteryx* may be related to modern flightless birds like the ostrich, its shoulder and wing suggest a closer relationship to enantiornithine birds from South America.

ON EMERGING FROM THE EGG that has protected it for several weeks, a hatchling *Gobipteryx* looks out on the harsh reality of the central Asian deserts. A sibling chick has already perished, but the parents, just overhead, are returning with food for the survivor.

The Hesperornithiform Birds

THE BIRDS RETURN TO THE SEA

HESPERORNIS

During the Cretaceous, some flying birds branched off from the main line of bird evolution and became such specialized swimmers that they lost their ability to fly. These birds, called hesperornithiforms, had teeth in their jaws, but otherwise resembled modern diving birds like grebes or loons. Again, convergent evolution explains the similar appearances arising from similar lifestyles. The bones of Cretaceous divers were thick and heavy enough to give their bodies the same density as water, so they would neither sink nor float when motionless. Their legs had moved far back on the body to a position well suited to propelling them through the water. Their legs, however, were locked in position behind the body and could not have been brought forward for walking. If these Cretaceous divers ventured on land, they must have slid on their stomachs, pushing themselves forward by undulations of their bodies. Modern seals use a similar technique to slide across the ice.

The skull of the Late Cretaceous diver Parahesperornis *(above) looks very primitive. The sharp pointed teeth set in a long narrow skull were well adapted to capturing fish. The lack of teeth at the front of the upper jaws indicates that a beak sheathed this region as it does in modern birds.*

The earliest known hesperornithiform is *Enaliornis,* discovered in 100-million-year-old rocks in England. More derived forms, including *Baptornis,* *Hesperornis* and *Parahesperornis,* lived during the Late Cretaceous in large saltwater bodies from Chile to the Canadian Arctic. Hesperornithiforms were rare by the end of the Cretaceous, and all disappeared with the dinosaurs 65 million years ago. One scientist believes they were driven to extinction by acanthopterygian fishes, which were becoming increasingly more successful as the toothed diving birds declined.

Hesperornis *(top),* Parahesperornis *(middle) and* Baptornis *(bottom) were three diving birds living in the seas covering Kansas during the Late Cretaceous.* Hesperornis *is the largest and most advanced hesperornithiform while* Baptornis *is the most primitive.*

The foot of Hesperornis *(left) resembles that of a cormorant, a modern diving bird (right). An example of convergent evolution, the feet of both birds evolved independently into paddles for propelling them through the water.*

Highly adapted to life at sea, hesperornithiforms were incapable of flying. Some discoveries show they ventured hundreds of kilometers from shore, leading some scientists to speculate that they gave birth to live young without ever visiting land. Other scientists believe hesperornithiforms nested in rookeries on isolated coastlines and islands in the Cretaceous seaways.

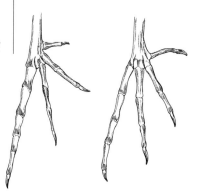

BAPTORNIS ADVENUS

Baptornis was a meter-long diving bird whose fossils have been recovered from the Upper Cretaceous rocks of Kansas, although a closely related form, *Neogaeornis*, has been recovered from Chile. *Baptornis* was more primitive than *Hesperornis* because its wings were longer, though clearly inadequate for flying. The wings of *Baptornis* helped it steer, though they could not have helped it "fly" underwater the way a modern penguin does. *Baptornis*, like other hesperornithiforms, used its feet for propulsion. Fossil footprints suggest its feet did not have webs like a duck's, but lobes like a grebe's. Coprolites, or fossilized dung, have been found with *Baptornis* and confirm its diet of small fish.

USING ITS LOBED FEET TO PROPEL itself rapidly underwater, *Baptornis* closes in on a school of fish. Unfortunately, the commotion has attracted the attention of a much larger predator, a shark, an animal virtually unchanged over hundreds of millions of years.

HESPERORNIS REGALIS

Like other hesperornithiform birds, *Hesperornis* was a flightless swimmer resembling modern cormorants (which may be descended from the pelican), grebes (a gruiform offshoot) and loons (descendants of shorebirds like curlews and killdeer). *Hesperornis* was more advanced than *Baptornis* because its front limbs were shorter, possibly making it a faster swimmer. The breastbone lacked a keel, but like other lower body bones, it was dense and heavy to help the animal sink quickly when diving and keep it from turning upside down. Special adaptations for high-speed swimming allowed the foot to rotate sideways as it was pulled forward, thus reducing resistance to its forward motion.

Othniel Charles Marsh collected the first *Hesperornis* specimen, consisting of only the lower part of a leg bone, in 1870 near Smoky Hill River in western Kansas. Extreme cold and the threat of hostile Indians prevented Marsh from looking for additional remains, but a field party returned the following year with a larger escort of troops. This time they found enough of a skeleton to establish *Hesperornis regalis* as a species.

Hesperornis is best known from Kansas, but it had a wide distribution that included Alaska, the Northwest Territories, Alberta, Manitoba, Wyoming, Montana and the Dakotas. So many specimens of juveniles were recovered near the Anderson River in the Northwest Territories that Dale Russell of the Canadian Museum of Nature suggested that the site must have been close to a nesting colony. In 1989, a Sino-Canadian expedition recovered *Hesperornis* neck vertebrae on Bylot Island off the north coast of Baffin Island in the Canadian Arctic. This locality also produced dinosaur bones. The Late Cretaceous climate in the Arctic would have been much more moderate than today, and fish would have been available year round in the open seas.

IN A KELP FOREST, A FISH seeks shelter from the early toothed diving bird *Hesperornis*. Highly active and maneuverable, the bird was the Cretaceous equivalent of the seal.

The
Palaeognathous Birds

THE EVOLUTION OF FLIGHTLESSNESS

CASSOWARY

*O*striches, cassowaries, emus, rheas and kiwis are modern flightless birds familiar to most readers. They are generally collected into a taxon called the Palaeognathae, which means "primitive jaws." The name refers to the arrangement of bones in the roof of the mouth, which is similar to the palate of a Late Cretaceous meat-eating dinosaur like *Tyrannosaurus*. Though palaeognaths descended from flying birds, most modern forms are flightless. Only modern tinamous from South America retain some limited ability to fly, and then only for very short distances. Many other species of birds independently lost their ability to fly, so not all flightless birds are palaeognaths. The dodo bird, for example, was really a gigantic ground-dwelling pigeon, and a flightless inhabitant of the Hawaiian islands is really a goose.

Most flightless palaeognathous birds lived within the past five million years, although one example, the Brazilian *Diogenornis fragilis*, dates back 50 million years. Because their palate is similar to a dinosaur's, scientists once speculated that palaeognaths evolved as a branch separate from all other birds. Similarities between an ostrich and an "ostrich-mimic" dinosaur seem to make this a distinct possibility. However, palaeognaths and neognaths share many derived characteristics not found in dinosaurs and therefore must have had a flying bird as a direct common ancestor.

Whether palaeognathous birds are interrelated is a more fundamental problem. Conceivably, some neognaths, with their advanced palates, lost their ability to fly and reevolved a primitive palaeognathous palate. However unlikely this may seem initially, in some modern birds, the roof of the mouth is palaeognathous in juveniles and neognathous in adults.

The moa was a palaeognathus bird from New Zealand. Because it became extinct less than a thousand years ago, many specimens have been found. Western scientists learned of the existence of moas in the 1830s, when Sir Richard Owen gave *Dinornis*, a spectacular example, its name.

Clues to the lifestyles of some extinct palaeognaths like the moa may be found by studying similar modern flightless birds. Fossil ostriches, for example, resemble modern ostriches, those amazingly swift-footed runners capable of reaching speeds of 80

The arrangement of bones in the roof of a palaeognath's mouth (top) is very different from a neognath's (bottom). The palaeognathous palate is primitive while the neognathous type, found in most modern birds, is more specialized. The roof of a neognath's mouth is more open, and the bones have more freedom to move, allowing neognaths to swallow larger chunks of food.

kilometers per hour. Moving in groups of up to 50 animals, modern forms eat fruits, seeds, plant matter, insects and small animals. Their wings have been reduced to a pair of small, almost useless limbs, which retain distinct claws. Like other fast runners such as antelope and deer, ostriches have only two functional toes on each foot.

Sir Richard Owen, the man who coined the word Dinosaur, *was also the first scientist to name a moa. Owen posed as a scale with the restored skeleton of* Dinornis *for one of his scientific publications.*

Other flightless birds like the gigantic elephantbirds, called the Aepyornithidae, reached three meters in height and weighed more than 400 kilograms, as much as four large men. Seven species lived on the island of Madagascar when humans arrived two thousand years ago, and some species survived into the tenth century. Elephantbirds' wings were tiny and useless, but their legs were pillarlike and massive. They could not reach the speed of ostriches, but they didn't need to. Their only natural enemies were the comparatively slow-moving crocodiles. Elephantbird eggs are still found in beach sands along lake shores. Natives once used the thick-shelled eggs to carry as much as 10 liters of fluid, a volume equal to seven ostrich eggs or 200 chicken eggs. One elephantbird egg has been recovered with the remains of an embryo inside.

The New Zealand kiwis are small palaeognathous birds with long curved beaks and tiny wings concealed by hairlike feathers. The nostrils at the tip of the bill are a unique characteristic not found in any other bird, and they are used to sniff out food on the ground. Kiwis lay huge eggs for their small size – a 3.5 kilogram female will lay a 450 gram egg. Although some palaeontologists have suggested kiwis are related to moas, the similarities appear to be the result of convergent evolution.

Small tinamous look similar to guinea fowl, but they have palaeognathous palates and seem closely related to the flightless rheas. Unlike other palaeognathus birds, tinamous have a keeled breastbone for the attachment of flight muscles, and their short wings can carry them for up to a hundred meters when they are alarmed. Most of the time, however, they act as though flightless and rely on camouflage for protection. The fossil record of tinamous stretches across five million years, and about 45 modern species inhabit Central America, Mexico and South America.

DINORNIS MAXIMUS

Moas were an unusual bird group living on the islands of New Zealand when humans arrived a thousand years ago. These large birds became easy game for the islanders, who soon drove the species to extinction. Moas had palaeognathous palates and superficially resembled ostriches. They had lost their wings, but retained a shoulder girdle. Moa feathers were similar to those found today in cassowaries. Moas also lost their pygostyles, the remnant of a backbone in the tail found in birds, probably because their tail feathers were no longer needed for flight. Their massive legs supported an enormous body weight, and the bones of the flat of the foot were short and heavy, with the toes splayed to form a broad foot for stability. Moas did not become swift runners like ostriches because no predators on the New Zealand islands were large enough to hunt them successfully.

The thirteen known species of moas can be assigned to two groups – the common Lesser Moas and the rare Greater Moas. The Lesser were no bigger than a large turkey, but one of the Greater Moas, *Dinornis maximus*, attained a height of three meters.

Because moas became extinct only recently, complete skeletons, feathers, skin, ligaments and even stomach contents have been discovered, most often in caves and swamps. Moas were well adapted to grazing or browsing on plants and had evolved to fill this niche because no mammalian plant-eaters competed with them. Like many birds, moas swallowed stones, some with diameters of up to five centimeters, to assist in the digestion of the tough vegetation they swallowed. Other New Zealand birds became flightless and shared the same food source.

In swamps, large moas were often bogged down by their great weight. In the Pyramid Valley Moa Swamp, discovered in 1937 on the South Island of New Zealand, palaeontologists found hundreds of moas that had died over a long period of time in an area smaller than most single-family houses. Many skeletons were found upright with their bones articulated.

SCREECHING IN ALARM, A 200-kilogram *Dinornis* struggles to free itself from the soft sticky mud of a swamp. But the more it struggles, the deeper it sinks. Its mate, unable to help, retreats to firmer ground.

An Unnamed Species from Montana

Fifty-million-year-old rocks in Montana have produced the remains of a yet-to-be-named palaeognathous bird described in the early 1980s. The Green River Formation of Wyoming, famous for its thousands of fossil fish, has yielded a similar species. The unnamed bird was less than half a meter tall. Unlike modern palaeognaths, it had well-developed wings with strong attachments to the shoulder girdle. The bony tail was short, much like a modern bird's.

One distinguishing feature, a bone in the lower jaw (called the splenial in reptiles), is large and very primitive in appearance. The presence of the splenial contradicts the suggestion that the palaeognathous palate evolved from the neognathous type, and that palaeognathous birds, like ostriches, had therefore descended from neognaths. This hypothesis arose because until the specimen from Montana was discovered the only birds with palaeognathous palates were less than five million years old.

CHASING A BEE for sport, this young unnamed bird from the Palaeocene of Montana tests the strength of its long legs and powerful wings.

The
Neognathous Birds

THE ADVANCED FLIERS

PRESBYORNIS

Most of the more than 8000 species of living birds have a neognathous palate and share a common ancestor. The earliest neognaths probably appeared in the Early Cretaceous, at least in North America. The first fossil records are mostly feather and footprint impressions, but enough bones exist to suggest that at least some modern bird families had evolved by the Late Cretaceous. By the Upper Eocene, about 40 million years ago, almost all modern families of neognathous birds had appeared, suggesting that an explosive phase of evolution occurred shortly after the extinction of their ancestors, the dinosaurs.

Early in their history, neognaths split into two fundamental branches – land birds and water birds. The most primitive land birds include the hoatzin, cuckoos, roadrunners, Old World vultures, eagles, hawks, falcons, game birds, pigeons and parrots. The Kingfishers, owls, swifts, hummingbirds, woodpeckers and more than 5000 species of songbirds represent more advanced land birds. Water birds include cranes, phorusrhacids, diatrymids, herons, storks, ibises, grebes, plovers, sandpipers, avocets, snipes, gulls, terns, auks, flamingos, ducks, swans, New World vultures, teratorns, pelicans, frigatebirds, boobies, cormorants, anhingas, albatrosses, petrels, loons and penguins.

Even in the most advanced neognathous birds, primitive dinosaurlike characteristics can still be detected, sometimes in individual species, sometimes in the group as a whole. The hoatzin's dinosaurian legacy, for example, can be traced in its ancient clawed hands, and virtually all advanced birds shows their dinosaurian ancestry in their scaly legs.

Footprints sometimes prove the existence of animals in places where bones were not typically fossilized. Aquatilavipes (top) from British Columbia and Ignotornis (bottom) from Colorado provide two examples of 120-million-year-old fossil impressions probably left by early neognathous birds. The footprints are very similar to modern shorebird tracks, but are different enough from each other to suggest that shorebirds were diverse during Early Cretaceous times.

A hoatzin hatchling's wings (top) are poorly developed, but its hands have distinct fingers with claws (bottom). As the animal matures, the hand loses its dinosaurlike appearance, the bones fuse and one of the claws is lost.

OPISTHOCOMUS HOAZIN

The hoatzin, a living bird from South America, is a very primitive neognathous bird whose closest relatives include cuckoos and roadrunners. *Hoazinoides magdalenae* is a species known from 5-million-year-old fossils collected in California's Magdalena Valley.

Hoatzin nestlings have two fingers with prominent functional claws on the leading edge of each wing. Many other birds have small claws on their hands when they are nestlings, but their feathers tend to hide them. A hoatzin chick uses its clawed fingers to almost crawl through bushes. As it matures, the hand bones fuse and the thumb loses its claw. With its wing fully-developed, it begins to walk only on its hind legs.

The hoatzin's diet, consisting mainly of arum leaves, requires that it have a very large crop to help it break down food for rapid digestion. Very few other modern birds feed on leaves because more time and storage space is required to digest plant fibers than seeds, fruit or meat. So hoatzins, like cattle, need enough digestive tract space to store the moistened leaves while bacteria break down the cellulose. Such a digestive system is heavy and cumbersome for a flying bird, which normally is as light as possible to enhance its flight capability.

USING ITS WINGS AS ARMS, A young hoatzin claws its way into the upper branches of a tree to escape the constricting coils of a deadly boa. An adult hoatzin, which no longer has claws on its front limbs, anxiously watches the snake from its perch.

©1991 J. Sovak

PHORUSRHACUS (PHORORHACOS)

Phorusrhacus (once better known as *Phororhacos*) is a well-known representative of a bird family related to living cranes and rails. This family lost the power of flight almost 40 million years ago, but retained short stubby wings. Some of the more than a dozen known species became towering predators standing as tall as three meters. The enormous skull, up to 48 centimeters long, had deadly jaws to kill and dismember its prey. Most species lived in South America, but they were successful enough to spread to North America and Europe. A discovery on Seymour Island in Antarctica shows one two-meter-tall form had even pushed that far south. The last phorusrhacid died out two million years ago.

Phorusrhacus is one of the few fossil birds to appear in a movie. In the 1961 Columbia Pictures production of Jules Verne's *Mysterious Island*, one of these giant birds attacks a party of people marooned on an island in the South Pacific. The animated model was convincingly brought to life through the technical wizardry of Ray Harryhausen.

LIFE IN A SOUTH AMERICAN forest has always been hazardous for small mammals. In an interesting role reversal, these early New World monkeys had little to worry about from this hungry flightless *Phorusrhacus* because they were the ones inhabiting the trees.

DIATRYMA GIGANTEA

Diatrymids lived on the northern continents of North America and Eurasia during the Early Tertiary, 45 to 55 million years ago. They are more closely related to phorusrhacids and modern cranes than to large modern ground-dwelling birds like ostriches. Many diatrymid species thrived, with one growing taller than an average man. Their legs, shorter and more massive than phorusrhacids', still allowed them to run rapidly.

Diatrymids inhabited an ecosystem without any real competition from large mammalian meat-eaters, but some scientists believe they were plant-eaters in spite of their enormous skulls and muscular jaws. Diatrymids may have replaced their forerunners, the predatory dinosaurs, although they eventually lost the evolutionary battle as modern families of large mammalian carnivores evolved in the Eocene.

AS A STORM APPROACHES THE marshes, *Diatryma* males engage in a ritualistic combat to establish dominance. Such battles are common in animals of all kinds and ensure that only the strongest and fittest males pass on their genes.

PRESBYORNIS

Duck-sized *Presbyornis* was a long-legged, web-footed flying bird that seems closely related to charadriiforme shorebirds. However, the skull is highly modified, and the braincase and bill are characteristic of ducks and swans. Other *Presbyornis* characters are known only in flamingos. The bill of *Presbyornis* was adapted for filtering algae and other plant material from the lake waters it foraged in 50 million years ago. *Presbyornis* represented an intermediate evolutionary stage between primitive shorebirds and modern ducks and flamingos.

Huge concentrations of *Presbyornis* skeletons were found in 1971 in Wyoming by a field party from the University of Wyoming. Bone and eggshell accumulations suggest *Presbyornis* lived in huge colonies, in which the young were raised and protected. Partial skeletons also have been found around the world, including Asia, Europe and South America, but they are not well preserved.

THE QUIET WATERS OF A LAKE MARGIN suddenly erupt next to a feeding *Presbyornis* as the crocodile makes its lunge. But the wary bird is too fast and makes its escape. Fifty million years ago, Wyoming was a semitropical paradise with extensive lake systems forming ideal habitats for *Presbyornis* and other shorebirds.

ARGENTAVIS MAGNIFICENS

Argentavis, exhumed from ten-million-year-old rocks in Argentina, had an estimated weight of 120 kilograms. Its 7.5-meter wingspan is the largest ever recorded for a bird. Before the description of *Agentavis* in 1983, no one believed a bird could become so large or heavy. *Argentavis* was a teratorn, a type of extinct bird closely related to New World vultures and storks. Other teratorns lived in the Los Angeles, California, region until recently, and their bones are often recovered from the La Brea tar pits.

Teratorns may have been fierce predators rather than scavengers like the vulture. Because their lower jaws were not fused, they could separate to allow the passage of huge chunks of food.

HOVERING *ARGENTAVIS* warily guards its victim from a pack of *Prothylacynus*, or borhyaenoid marsupials. This dominant meat-eating mammal, had more than met its match in a giant bird like *Argentavis*.

The Past Meets the Present

By this point, you've come face to face with some of the major discoveries and the lingering problems confronting palaeontologists as they seek to understand the origins of birds and pterosaurs and flight. You know that the massive creatures we normally think of as dinosaurs did not fly. Pterosaurs flew, but they were not dinosaurs. And there really are flying dinosaurs, but we call them birds.

But then again, classifications are a convenience invented by humans. Birds are now classified with the dinosaurs by many scientists, and if the definition of the term *dinosaur* were extended by only one step, it would encompass pterosaurs as well. Our understanding, like the creatures themselves, has evolved constantly. Palaeontologists once proposed that pterosaurs were derived from dinosaurs, and more than a century ago some believed that pterosaurs gave rise to birds. And they had their reasons. Pterosaurs, like birds and bats, were active fliers and not simply passive gliders. Like birds and some dinosaurs, they were warm-blooded, and at least the smallest forms were covered with hair to help them maintain the high constant body temperature necessary for an active predatory lifestyle.

Today, we recognize that the evolution of meat-eating dinosaurs shows a progression toward birds. Dinosaurs, for example, convergently evolved toothless beaks and other characteristics that made some look very birdlike. More than a hundred other characters shared by theropods and birds strongly indicate their close relationship. As you are now aware, scientists cannot always be sure whether some fossils are birds or theropods, and they think feathers may have evolved in theropods before birds incorporated them into their wing structure and took to the air. Remove the feathers of *Archeopteryx,* and you have a small carnivorous dinosaur.

Something about dinosaurs won't let our imagination rest. They were larger than life, and we return again and again to the hope that they may somehow have survived. And, in a very special way, they have. Before the great extinction marking the end of the Cretaceous, dinosaurs had prepared an evolutionary path for survival. The children of the dinosaurs may be easily spied on just about any day anywhere on the planet. When you watch songbirds gathered in a tree outside your window or pigeons congregated in a square in the heart of a city, you are watching the feathered warm-blooded descendants of the mighty dinosaurs. For at least half their history, they shared their world with the pterosaurs and dinosaurs.

We have learned much about "the flying dinosaurs," but we are challenged by how much more we have to learn. The debate on the origin of birds is far from over, and to a lesser extent this is also true for pterosaurs. Within pterosaurs, theropods and birds, hundreds of problems of relationship still need sorting out.

We continue to add new pages to the ever more complex scrapbook of the history of life on Earth. But an axiom of science is that every discovery brings with it new questions. Without doubt, thousands of fossilized pterosaur, dinosaur and bird species remain to be discovered. The often bizarre and always exciting twists of evolution already known may pale in comparison with what still remains hidden in the earth's crust. Our current knowledge of many species is based on incomplete or poorly preserved fossils, and better specimens must be recovered before we can answer even fundamental questions. For example, some baby animals look very different from their parents. Did pterosaurs, like duck-billed dinosaurs, lack head crests when they were babies? Try to imagine a baby *Pteranodon* without the large rudderlike crown. Why do some Late Cretaceous dinosaurs look more like modern birds than *Archaeopteryx*? Is this convergent evolution? Were some early birds relics from earlier times when birds branched off from theropods? Or were they really birds that had returned to the ground and lost their power of flight? And if so, why did they return to the ground? We have no clear answers yet.

The latest studies show dinosaurs had much more complex behavior than previously believed. Some moved in great herds, caring for their young as they migrated annually into the Arctic Circle to take advantage of the high plant productivity of a twenty-four hour polar summer day. Others collected at huge nesting sites to breed and raise their young. But we still know very little about the behavior of pterosaurs and the first birds. Were they social creatures? Did they congregate in flocks? Did they lay eggs in nests? When did the young leave their nests? Did the first birds migrate with the seasons? Again, we have no clear answers.

Pterosaurs, dinosaurs and birds are some of the the most fascinating actors in the play we call Life. Throughout millions of years, their roles have changed. The leathery-winged pterosaurs ruled the ancient skies during the acts we call the Triassic and Jurassic. But by the Cretaceous they were facing extinction. Dinosaurs lost the dominion of the land at the end of the Cretaceous, surrendering it to the mammals for reasons we don't understand. But dinosaurs did not make a final exit. Written into the script was their evolution into the elegant and versatile creatures we call birds.

Pronunciation Guide

Scientific names are often imposing to look at, difficult to remember and tongue-twisters to pronounce. They are simply names invented by scientists, but they have been latinized using Latin or ancient Greek roots. For example, *Tyrannosaurus rex* is formed from three words meaning "Tyrant Lizard King." Latin and ancient Greek are used because they are no longer in general use and therefore have no nationalist or political implications. So scientific names can be used internationally. *Tyrannosaurus rex* is spelled the same and looks the same in Chinese, English, Japanese or Russian publications.

The following is a phonetic guide to how I pronounce many of the more difficult names and terms used in this book. My pronunciation will not necessarily be exactly the same as that used by another palaeontologist. At one time it would have been important to use the correct Latin pronunciation of a name, but with the introduction of roots formed from the names of people and places from around the world, even this practice is no longer valid. For example, the name *Dsungaripterus* is a latinized combination of a Chinese place name (the Dsungar Basin of northwestern China) and the Greek word for finger (a suffix often used to indicate the fossil is a pterosaur). Using Chinese for the first part of the word and Greek for the ending, the pronunciation ends up being "Jung–ger–i–ter–us." The most important thing about how you say scientific names is simply to pronounce them so you are understood.

In the pronunciation guide, capital letters indicate stressed syllables, and bold letters indicate long vowel sounds.

Acanthopterygian – ak · en · THOP · ter · IJ · **e** · an

Acerosodontosaurus – A · sir · **OS** · **o** · DONT · **o** · SOR · us

Aepyornithidae – **a** · pe · **or** · NITH · **o** · d**e**

Alectrosaurus – e · LEK · tro · SOR · us

Albertosaurus – al · BER · to · SOR · us

Anurognathus – a · NYER · **o** · NA · thus ('th' as in 'think')

Apatornis – ap · at · OR · nis

Apatosaurus – a · PAT · **o** · SOR · us

Aquatilavipes – a · KWA · tel · **A** · vi · **pas**

Archaeopteryx – AR · k**e** · OP · ter · icks (popular pronunciation)

Archaeopteryx – AR · k**e** · **o** · TER · icks (scientific pronunciation)

Archaeornithomimus – AR · k**e** · or · NI · th**o** · **MI** · mus ('th' as in 'think')

Argentavis – AR · gent · **A** · vis

Avimimus – a · v**e** · **MI** · mus

Baptornis – bap · TOR · nis

Borhyaenoid – BOR · hi · EN · oid

Brachiosaurus – BRA · k**e** · e · SOR · us

Caenagnathus – ka · no · NA · thus

Carnotaurus – car · no · TOR · us

Cassowary – CAS · **o** · war · **e**

Coelurosauravus – se · LUR · e · sor · **A** · vis

Compsognathus – COMP · so · NA · thus ('th' as in 'think')

Conchoraptor – KON · ko · RAP · tor

Cosesaurus – KO · se · SOR · us

Cretaceous – kre · TA · shus

Ctenochasma – te · no · KAZ · ma

Deinonychus – di · NON · ik · us

Diatrima – di · a · TRI · ma

Didelphodon – di · DEL · fo · dawn

Dilophosaurus – di · LO · fo · SOR · us

Dimorphodon – di · MORF · **o** · dawn

Dinornis – di · NOR · nis

Diogenornis – di · **O** · jen · OR · nis

Diplodocus – di · plo · DO · kus

Dorygnathus – do · **re** · NA · thus ('th' as in 'think')

Draco – DRA · ko

Dromicieomimus – dro · **ME** · se · **o** · mi · mus

Dsungaripterus – jung · **GER** · i · **TER** · us

Elmisaurus – **EL** · mi · **SOR** · us

Enaliornis – e · **NAL** · **e** · **or** · nis

Enantiornithines – e · **NAN** · **te** · **or** · ni · th**e**nz

Eudimorphodon – **U** · **di** · **MORF** · **o** · dawn

Exocoetidae – ex · **o** · **SE** · te · **di**

Gnathosaurus – **NA** · th**o** · **SOR** · us ('th' as in 'think')

Gobipteryx – **GO** · b**e** · **TER** · icks

Hesperornis – **HES** · per · **OR** · nis

Hesperornithiforme – **HES** · per · **or** · **NITH** · i · form

Hoatzin – **HWOT** · sin

Hoazinoides – **HWOT** · zin · **OID** · **ez**

Hovasaurus – **HO** · va · s**or** · us

Huanhepterus – hwan · **HE** · ter · us

Icarosaurus – **IK** · a · ro · **SOR** · us

Ichthyornis – **IK** · th**e** · **OR** · nis ('th' as in 'think')

Ignotornis – ig · n**ot** · **OR** · nis

Ilerdopteryx – i · **LER** · **do** · **TER** · icks ('LER' as in 'hair')

Jurassic – jur · **AS** · ik

Kuehneosaurus – **KOO** · ne · **o** · **SOR** · us

Mesozoic – **ME** · zo · **ZO** · ik

Neogaeornis – ne · **o** · **gi** · **OR** · nis

Neognathous – ne · **o** · **NA** · thus ('th' as in 'think')

Opisthocomus – **o** · **PIS** · th**o** · **KO** · mus

Ornithischian – **OR** · ni · **THI** · sh**e** · an

Ornithomimus – **or** · ni · th**o** · **MI** · mus

Oviraptor – **O** · ve · **RAP** · t**or**

Pachyrhachis – pak · **e** · **RA** · kus

Palaeognathous -pail · **e** · **o** · **NA** · thus ('th' as in 'think')

Palaeocene – pa · **LE** · **o** · sen

Parahesperornis – **PAR** · a · **HES** · per · **OR** · nis

Parapholidophorus – **PAR** · a · **fo** · li · **do** · **FOR** · us

Phorusrhacus – **FOR** · us · **RA** · kus

Preondactylus – pre · on · **DAK** · ti · lus

Presbyornis – **PREZ** · b**e** · **OR** · nis

Protoavis – **PRO** · to · **a** · vis

Protoceratops – pr**o** · to · **SER** · a · tops

Psittacosaurus – si · **TAK** · **o** · s**or** · us

Pteranodon – ter · **AN** · **o** · dawn

Pterodactyl – ter · **o** · **DAK** · til

Pterodactyloid – ter · **o** · **DAK** · til · oid ('oid' as in 'void')

Pterodactylus – ter · **o** · **DAK** · til · us

Pterodaustro – ter · **o** · **DOW** · str**o** ('DOW' as in 'doubt')

Pterosaur – **TER** · **o** · s**or** ('TER' as in 'hair')

Quetzalcoatlus – **KWET** · zal · **KWA** · tel · us

Rhamphorynchoid – **RAM** · **for** · **ING** · koid ('koid' as in 'void')

Rhamphorynchus – **RAM** · **for** · **ING** · kus

Santanadactylus – san · tan · e · **DAC** · ti · lus

Scaphognathus – **SKA** · fo · **na** · thus

Saurischian – s**or** · **IS** · sh**e** · en

Saurornitholestes – s**or** · **OR** · ni · **THOID** · **ez**

Scelidosaurus – ske · **LID** · **o** · s**or** · us

Scleromochlus – skler · **MOK** · lus

Sordes – **SOR** · d**ez**

Struthiomimus – **STROO** · th**e** · **o** · **MI** · mus

Tarbosaurus – **TAR** · bo · **SOR** · us

Tertiary – **TER** · sh**e** · air · **e**

Theropoda – **THER** · **o** · **PO** · da

Titanopteryx – **TI** · tan · **o** · **TER** · icks

Triassic – tri · **AS** · ik

Troodon – **TRO** · **o** · dawn

Tropeognathus – **TRO** · pe · **o** · **NA** · thus ('th' as in 'think')

Tyrannosaurus – ti · **RAN** · **o** · **SOR** · us

Velociraptor – ve · **LOSS** · i · **RAP** · t**or**

Weigeltisaurus – **vi** · **GEL** · ti · s**or** · us

Where to Get More Information

For those wanting to learn more about pterosaurs, dinosaurs or birds, the following references are available from many public libraries or can be purchased from a book store. I have concentrated on bird and pterosaur references and books, which are not very common, and have mentioned only a few of the wide range of excellent books currently available on dinosaurs.

Carroll, R. L. *Vertebrate Palaeontology*. New York: W. H. Freeman and Company, 1988.

Feduccia, A. *The Age of Birds*. Cambridge, Massachusetts: Harvard University Press, 1980.

Hecht, M. K., J. H. Ostrom, G. Viohl and P. Wellnhofer, editors. *The Beginnings of Birds, Proceedings of the International Archaeopteryx Conference, Eichstatt, 1984*. Eichstatt, Germany: Freunde des Jura-Museums Eichstatt, 1985.

Heilmann, G. *The Origin of Birds*. New York: Dover Books, 1972 (reprint of D. Appleton and Company edition of 1927).

Langston, W., Jr. "Pterosaurs." *Scientific American*, February, 1981, pages 122-136.

Padian, K. "The Flight of Pterosaurs." *Natural History*, December, 1988, pages 58-65.

Reid, M. and J. Sovak. *The Last Great Dinosaurs*. Red Deer, Alberta: Discovery Books, Red Deer College Press, 1990.

Seeley, H. G. *Dragons of the Air*. New York: Dover Books, 1967 (reprint of D. Appleton and Company edition of 1901).

Swinton, W. E. *Fossil Birds*. London: British Museum (Natural History), 1958.

Weishampel, D. B., P. Dodson and H. Osmolska. *The Dinosauria*. Berkeley, California: University of California Press, 1990.

Pterosaurs and Fossil Birds:
Where to See Them

Pterosaurs and fossil birds can be seen in museums and even some parks around the world. This is not a complete list, and you will find most large natural history museums have at least some casts of the more spectacular pterosaurs and fossil birds.

AMERICAN MUSEUM OF NATURAL HISTORY, New York, New York. One of the finest dinosaur galleries in the world. A superb place to see the real skeletons of many theropods, including *Oviraptor, Albertosaurus* and *Tyrannosaurus.* Pterosaurs on exhibit include skeletons of *Pteranodon* and *Pterodactylus.*

BEIJING MUSEUM OF NATURAL HISTORY, Beijing, People's Republic of China. Excellent dinosaur displays and the first specimen recovered of the unnamed Lower Cretaceous bird from northeastern China.

BRITISH MUSEUM (Natural History), London, England. Many pterosaur remains on exhibit. Birds on display include *Archaeopteryx* and *Dinornis.*

CANADIAN MUSEUM OF NATURE, Ottawa, Canada. The fine dinosaur displays include skeletons of *Troodon*, the ornithomimid *Dromiceiomimus* and the tyrannosaurid *Daspletosaurus.*

CARNEGIE MUSEUM OF NATURAL HISTORY, Pittsburgh, Pennsylvania. Excellent displays of *Tyrannosaurus rex* and the pterosaurs *Campylognathus, Rhamphorhynchus, Pterodactylus* and *Pteranodon.*

CLEVELAND MUSEUM OF NATURAL HISTORY, Cleveland, Ohio. A nice dinosaur hall containing a mounted skeleton of *Diatryma.*

FIELD MUSEUM OF NATURAL HISTORY, Chicago, Illinois. A fine *Albertosaurus* on display in the Great Hall and a moa in the dinosaur hall.

GEOLOGICAL MUSEUM, University of Alberta, Edmonton, Alberta. A small but nice display including a *Pteranodon* skeleton from Kansas, bird footprints from the Upper Cretaceous and an excellent skull of the tyrannosaurid *Daspletosaurus.*

HAUF MUSEUM, Holzmaden, Germany. A small but beautiful museum most famous for the marine reptiles of the Holzmaden quarries, which have also produced the pterosaurs *Campylognathus* and *Dorygnathus.*

HUMBOLT UNIVERSITY MUSEUM OF PALAEONTOLOGY (part of the Museum of Natural History), Berlin, Germany. A superb collection of dinosaurs from Germany and eastern Africa. The Berlin specimen of *Archaeopteryx* and the feather from the same animal are housed here. Pterosaur specimens include *Dorygnathus.*

INSTITUTE OF VERTEBRATE PALAEONTOLOGY AND PALAEOANTHROPOLOGY, Beijing, People's Republic of China. A branch of the Chinese Academy of Sciences with the largest collections of vertebrate fossils in China, including pterosaurs, dinosaurs and birds. A new museum currently under construction will display such specimens as a full skeleton of *Dsungaripterus*, a troodontid from the Lower Cretaceous and the unnamed bird fossils from northeastern China.

JURA MUSEUM, Eichstatt, Germany. A small but lovely museum in the ancient monastery of Willibaldsburg, overlooking a beautiful Bavarian town. Displays include many fine pterosaurs from the nearby Solnhofen lithographic limestones such as *Rhamphorhynchus* and *Pterodactylus*, and one of the most complete specimens of *Archaeopteryx.*

LOS ANGELES COUNTY MUSEUM, Los Angeles, California. A cast of *Diatryma* is just one of the fossil birds fossils on display.

Museum National d'Histoire Naturelle, Paris, France. This beautiful old-style exhibition includes the pterosaurs *Campylognathus* and *Rhamphorhynchus*, and casts of *Compsognathus* and the tyrannosaurids *Tarbosaurus* and *Tyrannosaurus*.

Museum Ziemi, Warsaw, Poland. Mounted specimens of the ornithomimid *Gallimimus* and a skull of *Tarbosaurus* on display.

Orlov Museum of Palaeontology, Moscow, Russia. Perhaps the best palaeontological museum in the world. In addition to the nice selection of fossil birds are two specimens of the pterosaur *Sordes*, with the fur impressions preserved. Dinosaur displays include *Avimimus*, *Gobipteryx* eggs, *Velociraptor*, *Oviraptor*, *Gallimimus* and *Tarbosaurus*.

Page Museum of La Brea Discoveries, Los Angeles, California. Located at the La Brea tar pits, this gem includes displays of teratorn and other bird fossils.

Pyramid Valley Moa Swamp, New Zealand. More than 375 moas per hectare are estimated to be preserved at a site first discovered in 1937.

Royal Ontario Museum, Toronto, Ontario. One of the best dinosaur galleries in North America. Includes a mounted skeleton of the ornithomimid *Ornithomimus* and the tyrannosaurid *Albertosaurus*.

Royal Tyrrell Museum of Palaeontology, Drumheller, Alberta. Excellent dinosaur displays, including many theropods, are the strong point, but also on display are the oldest known bird footprints (*Aquatilavipes*) and bones of the toothed diving bird *Hesperornis*.

Senckenberg Natural History Museum, Frankfurt am Main, Germany. One of the best palaeontological displays in Europe. Includes beautiful specimens of *Rhamphorhynchus* and *Pterodactylus*, and the Eocene bat *Palaeochiropteryx*.

State Museum, Ulan Bator, Mongolia. Located near one of the richest sources of dinosaur skeletons in the world. Impressive dinosaur displays include *Avimimus*, *Velociraptor*, *Gallimimus* and four full skeletons of the tyrannosaurid *Tarbosaurus*.

Sternberg Memorial Museum, Hays, Kansas. *Pteranodon* is one of the many fossils displayed here.

Teyler Museum, Haarlem, the Netherlands. One *Archaeopteryx* skeleton was displayed here for many years with the pterosaurs.

United States Museum of Natural History (Smithsonian), Washington, D. C. In addition to skeletons of *Hesperornis* and *Teratornis* are many pterosaur skeletons from Kansas. Includes a life-sized model of *Quetzalcoatlus* from Texas. Also a good skeleton of the tyrannosaurid *Albertosaurus*.

University Museum, Oxford, England. A number of pterosaurs and dinosaurs on display.

Yale Peabody Museum of Natural History, New Haven, Connecticut. This magnificent old-style museum is an appropriate setting for some of O. C. Marsh's classic specimens. Dinosaurs such as *Deinonychus* and some giant sauropods share the exhibit halls with skeletons of *Hesperornis*, a moa, a dodo and *Pteranodon*.

Zigong Dinosaur Museum, Zigong, Sichuan, People's Republic of China. In addition to one of the most spectacular dinosaur displays in the world, an original specimen of the pterosaur *Angustinaripterus* is on display.

Systematic Index

New World monkey 142
New World vulture 139, 148

Old World vulture 139
Opisthocomus 140
Ornithischia 9
ornithischian dinosaur 9, 79-80
Ornithocheirus 39
Ornithodesmus 39
ornithomimid 88
Ornithomimus 81
ornithopod 79
ostrich 88, 131, 132
Oviraptor 12, 86, 96, 101, 122
owl 139

Pachycephalosaurid 79
Pachyrhachis 114
Palaeognathae 131
Palaeognathous bird 130, 131, 132,
   133, 136
Palaeognathous palate 131, 133,
   134, 136
Parahesperornis 125
Parapholidophorus 50
Parapsicephalus 39
parrot 139
pelican 74, 128, 139
penguin 139
Petaurus 20
petrel 139
Phobetor 70
pholidophorid 54
Phororhacos 142
phorusrhacid 139, 142, 144
Phorusrhacus 142
pigeon 107, 139
Plagiomenidae 20
Platydactylus 19
plesiosaur 33
plover 139
Preondactylus 32, 48, 50
Presbyornis 146
Prothylacynus 148
Protoavis 100, 101, 102
Protoceratops 84
Psittacosaurus 70
Pteranodon 28, 29, 37, 39, 42, 63, 72,
   76, 151
Pterodactyloidea 39, 40
pterodactyloid 40, 45, 62, 63, 70, 76
pterodactyl 40, 63, 70
Pterodactylus 32, 39
Pterodaustro 39, 64, 68
pterosaur 10, 11, 12, 15, 17, 19, 22,
   26, 27-76, 79, 80, 92, 97, 98, 108,
   150, 151

Q*uetzalcoatlus* (Ptexas Pterosaur)
   15, 29, 41, 63, 76

rail 142
Rhacophorus 19
Rhamphorhynchoidea 39, 40
Rhamphorhynchoid 45, 52, 63
Rhamphorhynchus 32, 39, 41, 42, 46,
   47, 54, 56, 58, 60
rhea 131, 133
roadrunner 139

Sandpiper 139
Santanadactylus 32
Saurischia 9
sauropodomorpha 80
Saurornithoides 90
saurischian dinosaur 79, 80
Saurornitholestes 12
Scaphognathus 32, 39
Scelidosaurus 52
Schoinobates 20
Scleromochlus 33, 34
seal 125, 128
shark 126
shorebird 37, 38, 117, 128, 139, 146
snake 10, 20, 98, 114, 120, 140
snipe 139
songbird 139
Sordes 32, 58
spoonbill 66
stegosaur 80
Stenonychosaurus 14, 15
stork 139, 148
Struthiomimus 88
sturgeon 37
swan 139
swift 139

T*arbosaurus* 92
teleost 54
teratorn 139, 148
tern 139
thecodont 33, 45, 96, 97
theropod 10, 11, 12, 79, 80, 81, 82,
   84, 88, 96, 97, 98, 101, 102, 104,
   120, 150, 151
Theropoda 80
tinamou 133
Titanopteryx 76
tree frog 58
Troodon 12, 14, 15, 81, 90, 97, 102
Tropeognathus 74
turtle 37, 114
Tyrannosaurus 12, 42, 79, 80, 81, 92,
   131

Unnamed Species from Argentina
   120
Unnamed Species from China 12,
   112
Unnamed Species from Montana
   136

Varanoid 114
Velociraptor 80, 81, 84, 90, 97, 122
vulture 38, 76, 139, 148

Weasel 80
Weigeltisaurus 24
wing lizard 29
woodpecker 139

General Index